DOG DAYS OF MURDER

COUNTRY COTTAGE MYSTERIES #2

ADDISON MOORE

BELLAMY BLOOM

BOOK DESCRIPTION

My name is Bizzy Baker, and I can read minds—not every mind, not every *time*, but most of the time, and believe me when I say it's not all it's cracked up to be.

A seminar on how to catch the perfect man is being held at the Country Cottage Inn, but with a killer on the loose, the only thing in store for the guests is a lesson on murder. Not only do I have another homicide on my hands, but Jasper's ex is in town and she's looking to take back what once belonged to her. It's October in Cider Cove. There's a fright around every corner and a killer closer than I'm willing to believe.

Bizzy Baker runs the Country Cottage Inn, has the ability to pry into the darkest recesses of both the human and animal mind, and has just stumbled upon a body. With the help of her kitten, Fish, a mutt named Sherlock Bones, and an ornery yet dangerously good-looking homicide detective, Bizzy is determined to find the killer.

Cider Cove, Maine is the premier destination for fun and relaxation. But when a body turns up, it's the premier destination for murder.

The Country Cottage Inn is known for its hospitality. Leaving can be murder.

CHAPTER 1

$\mathcal{M}$y name is Bizzy Baker, and I read minds. Not every mind, not every time, but it happens, and believe me when I say it's not all it's cracked up to be.

It's a crisp October evening and the inn is bustling with bodies. Every inch of the entry is dotted with pumpkins, and there are twin wreaths comprised of silk fall leaves hanging over the double door entry. The doors themselves remain open to accommodate the masses that are currently streaming their way in. To my right, there's a large banner strewn over the entry to the ballroom that reads *Welcome to the How to Snag a Man as Fast as You Can Seminar! Face it, honey, you're not getting any younger.*

And judging by the thick crowds swarming into the inn, there are a lot of women interested in how to snag a man despite the state of their crow's feet.

Nessa Crosby, my co-worker at the inn, bustles over. "I'm late! I'm so sorry, Bizzy. I was so excited about the seminar today that I didn't sleep last night. So, of course, I ended up taking a nap and well, I overslept." She wrinkles her nose as she hands me her purse. "Please put this in the cabinet down below."

"You bet," I say, doing just that while she secures her name badge over her blouse.

Nessa Crosby is a beautiful brunette with bronzed skin and a lightning white smile. She's been working for me at the inn ever since she graduated from college last summer. I've known both her and her sister, Vera, forever, mostly because they're blood-related to my best friend. Vera and I went to high school together, where she thought it would be a good idea to start horrific rumors about me. And even though Nessa didn't care for me by proxy, we've slowly grown closer.

Working elbow to elbow next to someone for a year solid can mend a lot of fences—or tear them down. Thankfully, for our sanity we've chosen the former.

A stunning redhead smiles wide at the two of us just as Nessa jumps behind the reception counter and lands by my side.

"Welcome to the Country Cottage Inn," I say to the well-polished woman before us. She's donned a bright red power suit and holds an adorable black and white puppy in her hands—cute enough to melt my soul into a puddle of puppy-loving mush. "How can I help you today?"

"I'm Ginger King." It comes out curt and a touch snooty as if her name should say it all—and oddly enough, tonight, it does just that. Her lips pull into a tight line as she examines me. *Good thing I'm here. A mousy girl like this needs all the help she can get in the male department.*

A breath hitches in my throat as I try not to audibly gasp.

That's the thing about reading minds. You never really want the general public to know what you're capable of.

I can't help but take umbrage at the thought. I certainly don't need help in the *male* department as she called it. I just so happen to be dating a brilliant homicide detective—and Jasper Wilder is a gorgeous one at that. In fact, he's right upstairs helping his mother get settled in. Her townhouse suffered an unfortunate plumbing issue and she'll be staying at the inn for some time. I've yet to meet her, but I just know it will be the highlight of my night.

An instant frown takes over my features as I study the beautiful, yet demeaning redhead before me. That adorable puppy tucked in her arms shivers and whimpers, and I can't help but feel sorry for the poor creature, considering who's holding him.

I try to pry into the poor pooch's mind, but there's nothing but static going on in there. Most likely a sign of fear.

Knew it. Ginger here is nothing but a detriment to the poor thing.

My head tips up a notch because I have a feeling I'm about to take it on the chin.

"How can I help you, Ms. King? I'm Elizabeth Baker. Please feel free to call me Bizzy." I force a smile.

Ginger King, self-help guru, blogger, and influencer extraordinaire, happens to be the grand dame of tonight's flirtatious festivities. And seeing that I'm the manager of the Country Cottage Inn, it's my job to ensure all of her deepest, darkest, perhaps even shallowest desires are met. I have a feeling her desires are far more familiar with that last category the most.

"Help me?" She blinks back with a laugh caught in her throat. *Please. As if I would take a word of advice this frazzled thing could offer.* "Why, I'm here to help *you*—help you both." She chortles away as she looks from me to my co-worker, Nessa Crosby, as we stand at the reception counter.

Ginger flashes her jewel-tone emerald eyes at Nessa and me. "I'm here to ensure you that every staff member interested in joining my seminar tonight will have *free* all-access entry. I'll make sure to let the girls working the registration tables know."

Fish jumps onto the marble counter, traverses a few tiny pumpkins we have on display as an homage to fall, and ambles up next to me. *I'd steer clear if I were you, Bizzy.*

I give a tiny nod to the cute little cat. Fish is my sweet black and white long-haired tabby that I found a few months back near my sister Macy's soap and candle shop, Lather and Light. Of course, I can read the minds of animals, too, almost always better than I can with people. They always have fascinating things to say. And I have a feeling Fish is right. I should definitely stay away from anything Ginger has to offer. Have I mentioned Fish is full of sage advice?

"Free all-access pass?" I'm almost amused. "Wow, that's wonderful, Ginger." I shrug. "I appreciate all you've done for the inn already." It comes out lackluster, but I couldn't help it. All she's done is cause outright chaos, but I subscribe to the golden rule in business. The customer is always right. "Would you like me to watch your dog while you give the presentation? We have a wonderful pet care facility, right here on the premises."

She jerks the puppy away as if I were ready to snatch it. "Heavens no. Peanut never leaves my side. He's my baby, if you know what I mean." She makes a face at the pudgy little angel. *This bag of fleas isn't my anything. He's Shelby's problem. I'm just thankful all I need to do is hold the mutt for an hour. Shel was right. Having a creature glued to my side makes the masses gravitate to me all the more.* She rolls her eyes at the thought, and my mouth rounds out in horror.

I clear my throat. "Well, my kitten is my baby as well, so I know what you mean." That is, if you meant what you said. "What kind of a dog is he?" Whoever this Shelby person is, she's insane for giving custody of her tiny treasure to this monster for five minutes, let alone an hour.

She glances to the ceiling. *What did Shel say again?* She snaps her fingers my way as if her scripted answer was coming back to her.

"French Bulldog mixed with terrier," she's quick to blurt it out. "I don't do breeders. I get all of my dogs from the pound." It comes out wooden like a bad actress reciting her lines. "I'm a rescuer at heart." *As if.* "Which brings me to my next point. I'd like to rescue every last female employee of this dreary inn"—a maniacal grin threatens to break out over her face—"from their equally dreary love lives." *And that is indeed the truth.*

A jumble of words catches in my throat.

First off, the inn is far from dreary—with the exception of the coastal fog, which most people, including myself, find just delightful.

The Country Cottage Inn just so happens to be set on beachfront property in cozy Cider Cove, Maine. The inn has been one of the state's official premier destinations for fun and relaxation going on four years now—the exact amount of time that I've been running the place. Coincidence? I think not.

Second of all—what makes her think our love lives are so dreary? I don't see a hot detective attached to her side. I'm getting the feeling Ginger here is a know-it-all. And if she really knew it all, I think she'd see there's more to the world than meets her beady little, narrow-minded, far too judgmental eyes.

And there's definitely more to that sweet little peanut in her arms than meets the eye. I think the dog's owner was afraid to tell her the tiny pooch might be a Pit Bull mix. I have a feeling Ginger would drop him like a hot *pooch*-tato if she knew. What most people don't realize is that Pitties make excellent pets.

"Rescue *me*!" Nessa gives an animated squeal, and I can't help but frown over at her. "I just can't believe *the* Ginger King is here!" she riots it out as if the words were begging to burst from her all along. "You're *really* here! Standing here at the reception desk of my dreary little inn. And you're so right about the dreary thing. We hardly ever see the sun in this part of Maine. And I just know you'll be right about everything you're about to say tonight, too. I wouldn't miss it. In fact, I'll be taking copious notes. Oh, who am I kidding? I'm so in love with your little Peanut. I doubt I'll take my eyes off him." Nessa does an odd little hop. "I can't believe you're letting us in for *free*." She grabs ahold of my hand and gives it a death squeeze. "Can you believe it, Bizzy? It's our lucky night!" She sucks in a quick breath as she reverts her attention to the charlatan at hand. "Can I get you to sign a copy of your book for me? I loved every page of *How to Snag a Man as Fast as You Can.* And I love the tagline, too—*Face it, honey, you're not getting any younger.* I brought my copy with me tonight, and I've read it cover to cover twice now." She winces. "Okay, so I might have read it more like twelve times, but I'm determined to follow all of your principles and land the very best man that I can. I'm especially interested in those that fall under the category of men of a certain caliber."

Ginger smirks over at poor Nessa who seems to have unraveled at the seams in a fit of unwarranted adulation.

She shakes her head. *Oh, sweetie, I have a feeling you'll have to read it fifty times, if not one hundred, to even hope to stand a chance with a man of a certain caliber.*

My mouth falls open at her brazen—albeit private—insult.

Ginger twists her crimson-stained lips. "It will be my pleasure to sign the book for you, Nessa." She turns my way. "Of course, I'll gift you a signed copy as well." *And I have a feeling if Bizzy here put the whole book into a blender and drank it, there would still be far too much work to do. Lord knows I don't specialize in miracles.*

A choking sound emits from my throat. "That's very kind of you to offer," I say. "But I already have a man of a certain caliber."

Fish nods as if agreeing. *You tell her, Bizzy. And tell her I've got a dog of a certain caliber, too! We don't need her or her silly book to rule our lives.*

And that dog that Fish is so quick to claim is Jasper's pooch, a sweet mixed breed named Sherlock Bones. Fish and Sherlock didn't always see eye to eye, but they're definitely coming around.

Nessa shakes her head my way. "No, I don't think you do, Bizzy. Jasper is just a detective. I'm pretty sure detectives don't earn a seven-figure income. Face it, he's not a man of a certain caliber."

Oh—*that* caliber. I get it.

I openly make a face at Ginger. A man of a certain caliber is code for a man of a certain financial standing.

Ginger laughs as if it were the funniest thing in the world, and her green dress sparkles in the light. Obviously, the color represents greed.

I cast a quick glance at the throngs of beautiful young women streaming in at an unimaginable pace. My goodness, they're both man *and* money-hungry. And ironically, they're about to be swindled out of a hundred and twenty dollars a pop.

Honestly, when I heard Ginger King wanted that much money for a person to sit and listen to her man-trapping tips, I thought she might garner an audience of twenty if she was lucky. I'd better call the café in the back and let them know to amp up production for the refreshment table. After Ginger attempts to hypnotize the masses, there will be a reception to follow.

Ginger leans in toward Nessa. "Not to worry. Income was simply a footnote as far as any of the categories went." *Heaven help her if she believes that. If I had my way, any tips about income should have been highlighted and printed in bold.*

I crimp my lips at her for the thought. I figured as much. Ginger is nothing but a gold digger, and she's happily selling picks and shovels to help others follow along in her gold-digging ways.

"A *footnote*?" Nessa looks crestfallen at the thought. "Oh well, I'm still shooting for the green gold." She gives Ginger a cheeky wink. "Don't tell anyone, but I highlighted those passages and they're some of my favorite lines from your book."

Ginger laughs once again—just the way she's laughing all the way to the bank.

"Don't *you* tell anyone"—she leans in and whispers—"those are my favorite lines, too. Don't be late to the seminar. Afterwards, there will be drinks with Carter O'Riley and men from the O'Riley Organization. What's better than a handful of strappy, beefy singles ready to mix and mingle?" She pauses to look my way. "I can't teach these ladies to fish and not offer a few sexy men in a barrel." She cackles once again. "Remember"—she points a blood red fingernail at Nessa—"a man isn't off the market until he's got a ring on both your finger and his. If you find a piece of prime meat you want to sink your fangs into and he has a loose attachment, you keep right on biting in his direction. That's still fertile ground, I tell you."

"A loose attachment?" I shake my head at all the loveless lingo. "Like a tool belt?"

Both Ginger and Nessa share a laugh at my expense.

Nessa doesn't waste a second before shoving her elbow into my rib. "A loose attachment is a girlfriend, Bizzy. Get with it."

"A girlfriend?" I gasp at the thought. This shyster is teaching women to steal *other* women's men! That is so not okay.

Dear Lord. Is it too late to give Ginger Gold Digger King and all her money-grabbing minions the boot?

I glance to the stairwell and can't help but feel as if Jasper is in more danger than I thought. Something tells me a drop-dead gorgeous homicide detective could be a rather hot commodity in a room full of wedding-hungry women—seven-figure income or not. And apparently, *girlfriend* or not, too.

Hey? Maybe I can convince him to stay in his mother's room for the night.

"I'll see you ladies inside." Ginger gives us a three-fingered wave as she takes off in the direction of the ballroom.

"Wait!" Nessa sags with defeat as Ginger is quickly mobbed by the crowd. "I didn't even get to tell her I went to college with her friends." She tosses a hand in the air. "Kevin Bacon was right when he said there was less than six degrees of separation between us all."

"I don't think Kevin Bacon actually said that." I crane my neck in an effort to get a better look at the stairwell once again.

Jasper's probably about done with helping his mother settle in. I'll admit, I'm not too thrilled with the idea of my drop-dead gorgeous quasi-boyfriend roaming the ground while this place is crawling with desperate women—who, by the way, are encouraged to sink their fangs into any man without a ring.

The nerve.

If I had known about these less than savory dating shenanigans Ginger is pushing, I wouldn't have agreed to book the seminar in the first place.

"Bizzy!" My best friend, Emmie, trots this way, dressed a little fancier than usual for her job as the manager of the Country Cottage Café. It's a large restaurant in the back of the inn, attached with a sunroom that looks right over at the Atlantic.

Emmie leans in with her wavy shoulder-length dark hair and her frosty blue eyes shining like beacons. Emmie—*short for Elizabeth*—Crosby and I have been friends as far back as I can remember. Seeing that we had the same first name, we decided to stick with our nicknames, and that's all we've ever been known as ever since. Emmie and I share the same dark hair and pale blue eyes, which often prompted people to believe we were sisters. We *are* sisters—just not blood-related.

"Bizzy, I left the kitchen going with a skeleton crew. One of Ginger's assistants just came back and let us all know we were welcome to sit in on the seminar." She sings that last part. Emmie is prone to sing when she gets a little too excited. "I hope I can get a refund on that ticket I bought."

"You bought a ticket?" I squawk. "Emmie, this woman is a scammer. You wouldn't believe the terrible things I just heard her say. I'll make sure you get your money back."

Nessa all but muzzles me with a hiss, and Fish hisses right back at her as if coming to my defense.

"Oh, stop." Emmie wrinkles her nose. "I need a man, Bizzy. And believe me, I'm doing all the research I need in order to get one." She flattens her hands over her little black dress. "Word on the street is, she's supplying a buffet of fresh meat after the event. I gotta run." She backtracks a moment. "Oh, and Fish?" She gives my little kitten a sly wink. "The chef may have spilled a bag full of trash behind the building. Cod was on the lunch menu," she trills as she takes off. Even though Emmie has no idea I can read minds, nor that I can communicate with my sweet cat, it hasn't stopped her from talking to Fish herself.

Fish hops off the counter and makes a mad dash for the exit.

"Fish!" I call out. "You don't eat trash!"

I do when there's cod involved.

And just like that, she's gone.

Fish has a brass nametag around her neck, yes, in the shape of her playful moniker, and she's well-known as the inn's pet mascot. I'm proud to say that the Country Cottage Inn is a pet friendly establishment, and we even have a fully functional pet sitting facility out back known as Critter Corner.

An older woman with long gray hair and a flowing purple kaftan runs up looking every bit frazzled, and yet adorably so. The woman in question just so happens to be Georgie Conner, a familial castoff from one of my father's many divorces.

Nathan Baker's vast collection of wives has come and gone, but for some reason, this once upon a mother-in-law has stuck around in our lives, and I couldn't be happier about it. In fact, I let her stay in one of the over three dozen cottages that belong to the inn.

Georgie Conner is the only living being I've told about my ability to pry into other people's thoughts.

"Bizzy Baker." Her steely blue eyes narrow to slits. "How dare you not tell me there was a portal into the male mind afoot this evening." She shakes a crumpled flyer for the event my way. "I happened to find this on my doorstep on my way to break a bag full of bottles." Georgie is an artist who specializes in glass mosaics. In fact, the Cider Cove City Council has hired her to do a giant mural along the north side of Main Street, and she's been happily smashing glass ever since.

I can't help but make a face. "I didn't tell you because I didn't think you'd be interested."

"Oh, I'm interested." She pulls out a tube of lipstick from her purse and gives her mouth a quick swath of purple. "At my age, you need all the help you can get." She dashes off before I can remind her she looks great for her age, despite her insistence to reek of questionable patchouli products procured from my sister's shop.

Speaking of my sister, both she and my mother stride my way looking as if they were about to paint the town red with regret. Macy has dyed her dark locks blonde and wears it in a bob that just dusts her neck. Macy is older than me by a year and has always been far more cunning and quick to employ her sarcastic superpowers on whomever she chooses.

A small rush of patrons head this way simultaneously and Nessa begins processing them in haste. I'm guessing her need for speed has everything to do with the fact doors for the seminar will be closing soon.

Macy widens her eyes a moment as she looks my way. "You have to get someone to cover and join us."

Mom offers a furtive nod. "This is going to be big, Bizzy."

"This is going to be a disaster." I frown over at my mother. My mother, Ree Baker, is a beauty queen at any age with a svelte figure that can rival either of her daughters, dainty cut features, and warm blue eyes. But she's as fierce a businesswoman as they come. She just retired from her real estate empire not too long ago, but rumor has it, she still does her best to nosey around the office. Currently, she's making it a practice to help my sister out at Lather and Light, the aforementioned shop Macy would rather burn down than run. But it fell into my sister's lap when she needed it the most, so she continues to slog along. Macy has always been better suited for Wall Street rather than Main Street.

"Mom," I moan. "Please tell me you're not into this, too."

"Nope." She pulls out a silver compact and checks her look in the mirror. "I've got me a good man." She gives a sly wink, and I wince because I happen to know that she's dating Jasper's brother, Maximus Wilder. He owns his own restaurant in Seaview. Although at the moment, only Mom and I know that she's dating Jasper's brother. I haven't even confessed the familial malfeasance to Jasper yet.

Mom stretches her lips back as far as they'll go in a mocking smile to my sister. "I'm just here supporting my daughter in an endeavor to learn all about the male species."

"Yes, well," I grunt. "Believe me, you'll want to unlearn it as quickly as you can." I pull out a few ID badges from the drawer beneath me. "Here, show them these, and give one to Georgie, too. They'll let you in for free. The last thing we want is to pay for this catastrophe."

They take off just as a trio of pretty girls heads this way. They all look to be somewhere in age between Nessa and me. And since Nessa is in her early twenties and I'm mid-to-late, that sounds about right.

There's a strawberry blonde with her hair in an adorably messy bun, a sweet brunette with a tiny nose and big pouty lips, and a copper-haired girl with a short precision cut that sits just underneath her ears. The copper-haired girl's eyes keep flitting around as if she were expecting to see someone in the crowd. She looks shifty and altogether uncomfortable.

Nessa gasps at the sight of them as she flags them down. The copper-headed girl on the end gives a slight wave and shouts that they'll catch her inside before they speed off to the registration table.

Nessa leans in. "That's Chelsea, Shelby, and Scout Pratt. Those are the friends that I went to school with." She says *friends* with air quotes. "They're the ones that know Ginger. Chelsea and Shelby both run really successful socials." She wrinkles her nose as if the idea disgusted her.

"Socials?" I shake my head while still looking in the direction of the girls.

"Yup. Social media. They're some of the most sought-after influencers on the planet." She sighs. "And poor Scout. Chelsea and Shelby pretty much hazed her last year. She was just getting out the gate as an influencer and was high in demand until Chelsea and Shelby pulled a few stunts. It was all in fun, but after the disaster that ensued, Scout had to give up her dreams of being an influencer. Believe me, no one is crying for her. She opened up a PR company and landed Ginger King as her first client. I really do like Scout. But don't get me started on how I feel about Shelby Harris. Now there's someone I wish I never had to see again." Nessa turns and offers a spastic wave to Grady Pennington, our other co-worker, who just so happened to walk through the door. "Grady's here to man the fort. I'll see you inside, Bizzy."

She takes off just as Grady, a dark-haired Irish god, as the girls around here like to call him, takes over at the helm. Grady, too, came to the inn after graduating from college last year, and he's been an invaluable employee ever since. Both he and Nessa keep telling people this is just a stepping stone in their lives, but I've grown so used to them I'd hate to see either of them step away anytime soon.

"*Mmm mmm.*" Grady shakes his head with an approving, somewhat greedy, grin blooming on his lips as he looks to the crowd thick with beautiful women. "Is it my birthday, Bizzy? Because you really didn't have to go overboard with the pretty girls. It's not against the law for me to demand their phone numbers, is it? I mean, of course, I'll be needing their numbers for official inn business."

"How about you just mind your own business?" I laugh as I give him a quick rundown on those who have checked in and those who are checking out before I step around the counter and join the thick crowd milling around in the lobby.

The Country Cottage Inn feels every bit my own, but it happens to belong to a wealthy earl in England. He pays me to run the place as if it were my own, and I do just that. I love every last inch of this beautiful place. And the inn is just as stately inside as it is outside with its stone façade and its blue shutters adorably ensconcing each of the many windows. Ivy runs up over every speck of the exterior, giving it a true Ivy League appeal. The estate sits on a vast acreage and boasts of over thirty cottages that we rent out as well. I happen to live in one as does Emmie— and as does my quasi-boyfriend, Detective Jasper Wilder. Jasper recently transferred to the neighboring town of Seaview after he had an abrupt breakup with his girlfriend.

Another robust crowd streams into the inn, and a part of me wonders if we're breaking fire code with all of these dolled-up bodies. I can feel my stress levels start to go up, and I cringe because I know what's coming.

I could just kill.

When I get my hands on her.

If only I can land myself a sugar daddy.

A bevy of voices go off at once in my head. It's exactly what happens when I'm stressed. I hear every thought in the vicinity.

Thankfully, it's nothing I deal with on a daily basis, but something tells me that until Ginger King and her minions vacate the property, I'll be listening in on one too many internal conversations all at once.

For the last time—

I hope they have at least one man who knows how to use his tie.

I gasp at that last one as the mental snippets come in faster and faster.

There will be heck to pay.

Won't get away with it.

"Bizzy Baker?" an all too familiar deep voice strums from behind, but before I can turn around, his spiced cologne permeates my senses as his arms find their way around my waist. He lands a soft kiss to my cheek before I spin in his arms and take in this six-foot-two, dark-haired, gray-eyed deity.

Jasper and I haven't openly discussed being an official couple, but we sure do enjoy spending all of our free time together glued at the lips. You'd think we were training for the kissing Olympics the way we've been going at it—and believe me when I say, we would definitely medal. And who could blame me for training so hard? Jasper Wilder is a god among men.

A slight titter goes off in the crowd as the women around us stop in their tracks to ogle him.

A whistle goes off near the ballroom, and soon everybody in the foyer drains in that direction.

"Careful," I say, hiking up on my tiptoes and gifting him a kiss on the lips. "You're causing a scene."

A warm laugh strums through his chest before it stops abruptly and his eyes widen as he looks to something at the door.

I follow his gaze to find a stunning woman with long, wavy, dark hair, eyes that shine like fiery ambers, and a face that has probably graced every magazine cover from here to France—she's just that beautiful.

The woman stops cold once she spots Jasper and their eyes lock for a moment before she quickly takes off for the registration table and hustles into the ballroom herself.

"Jasper, do you know her?" I ask.

She looked angry with him, or terrified to see him, or both, but I don't dare say that out loud.

"Yes, I do." His muscles tense around my waist for a moment. "That's Camila Ryder."

My heart sinks at the thought of Jasper knowing such a beautiful woman—and the fact he still seems stunned to see her doesn't make me feel all that great either.

"Can I ask as how you know her?" I keep my voice steady as I try not to freak out. And yet something in me is demanding to do just that.

Jasper twists his lips with a look of disdain. "She's my ex-girlfriend."

I hold my breath for a second.

"Your *ex*? The one that left you for your best friend?" My fingers pop to my lips, but it's too late. I've already unleashed the words. And yes, that's exactly what happened. Jasper's ex hightailed it out of his life for best friend pastures. A totally unkosher thing to do. I say good riddance.

"That's the one." He shakes his head as he wraps his arms around me tightly. *The last person on earth I wanted to see here tonight.*

I glance in the direction of the ballroom, trying my hardest to see if I can pick up on her thoughts, but it's just a jumbled choir of voices.

She'll have to go.

This had better work.

I'll want my money back if I don't land a decent catch.

I'll have to kill her.

I crimp a wry smile up at Jasper.

Something tells me the rest of the evening will be murder.

CHAPTER 2

The ballroom of the Country Cottage Inn is buzzing with excitement as Ginger King stands at the front of the room, holding sweet little Peanut in her arms as she preaches and teaches about all things bawdy and slightly distasteful.

Mayor Mackenzie Woods made the introduction, and that put a sour taste in my mouth right at kickoff. Mack and I used to be friends until she all but tried to drown me in a whiskey barrel when we were kids. And it just so happens that soon after that oxygen-deprived, panic-inducing event, I've had the strange ability to pry into other people's minds. I also have Mack's whiskey barrel attack to thank for the fact that I'm terrified of bodies of water and confined spaces. But despite her effort to snuff me out—accidentally she says—our friendship hobbled on right up until high school where Mack saw fit to steal every one of my boyfriends. Suffice it to say, we weren't friends for very long after that.

Rows and rows of white ladder-back chairs have been set up here in the ballroom, and each one is filled with a warm, beautiful, mostly youthful body.

Ginger has been rambling on and on, giving all her best tips and tricks on how to snag a man. So far they consist of suggestions to whiten your teeth, find a medical spa that will inject botulism into your face in an effort to paralyze your wrinkles into submission, take a small loan to buy out the beauty counter at your local mall, and piece together a wardrobe that consists of leather and lace. But the meat and potatoes is offered up at the end when she brazenly suggests women go after much older men—preferably those with money.

"Stalk the man you're interested in, show up where he shows up," she chants, much to the enthusiastic applause of the room.

Ginger goes on to extrapolate on the finer points of ambush dating—that's where the stalking comes in.

Is he enjoying his coffee alone? Join him.

At a bar having a drink? You make sure you're right there next to him.

And let's not forget the lip plumping, the intense hair color analysis, and the ridiculous six-inch stiletto requirement.

In my opinion, a woman should only do any of those things if she wants to—and only for herself. Sure, I've whitened my teeth and chosen an outfit that I thought looked vampish a time or two —but I didn't do it in an effort to snag a millionaire. Okay, fine. I did it in an effort to snag a homicide detective, but Jasper was well worth a high heel or two.

And speaking of millionaires—that's another thing Ginger expounded to the masses. Millionaires are no longer a hot commodity. Apparently, you can find a run-of-the-*mill* millionaire driving around in a sedan while wearing argyle sweaters.

I had to roll my eyes at that one. I happen to like both sedans and argyle sweaters, and I couldn't care less that Jasper wasn't rolling in billions.

Macy jumps out of her seat and heads to the refreshment table in the back, so I give Jasper a quick pat to the knee before following her over.

I can't believe I invited Jasper to join me.

What was I thinking?

He's going to laugh for a year straight after listening to this bobble-headed brainwashing taking place. Not that I could blame him.

Macy snaps up a handful of the pumpkin spice mini muffins the Country Cottage Café delivered fresh and hot. Emmie and I thought up the recipe ourselves.

All my life I've wanted to be a baker, and considering my surname, it only seemed natural. But, unfortunately, I'm anything but natural in the kitchen. I tend to burn, undercook, or on rare occasions, both, anything I attempt to create—and honest to goodness, that itself seems to take a talent. But it doesn't stop me from trying my hand at baking up a sweet treat.

"Can you believe this?" Macy whispers as she nods to the front where Ginger seems to be wrapping up her psychotic spiel. "It's like a coven in here, featuring all the prettiest witches Maine has to offer."

"Funny," I say. "You're not really buying into the spell she's casting, are you?"

"Are you kidding?" My feisty sister's eyes bug out. "I've already downloaded the audio book so I can play it on a loop. I'm thinking about having it on while I sleep. You know, letting it sink in on a subliminal level. Do you know who's not buying into it?"

"Me," I deadpan and she makes a face.

"No." Macy gives me the crazy eyes. "Our mother. Can you believe she has a boy toy to call her own? And here I am single and desperate to mingle." She pops a mini muffin into her mouth and chews with haste. "I can't wait to meet him at the Haunted Harvest Festival tomorrow. I'm not sure who's more excited, her or me. I bet he's old and wrinkly and has a bank account loaded with dead presidents." She pops another pumpkin spice mini muffin into her mouth and moans as she heads back to her seat.

"Dead presidents?"

A riotous applause breaks out, and soon enough the bodies are circulating throughout the room. Emmie's pumpkin spice mini muffins start disappearing at an alarming rate, and it only pleases me to see it. I'll have to do a refill run quicker than anticipated. I'd say they were a bigger hit than Ginger and her manhandling ways—but, seeing that there's a thick crowd mobbing her at the moment, I doubt others would agree with me.

Georgie runs up with her purple kaftan flowing behind her, a huge rather naughty looking grin on her face.

"Can you believe it, Bizzy?" she beams as she snatches up a few pumpkin spice mini muffins herself. Her gray hair is wild and wiry and adds an all-around charming granny appeal. "Every pot has a lid! Ginger said it herself. You can't make that stuff up."

"*Please.*" I can't help but avert my gaze. "She didn't have to make a single thing up. She borrowed every tired adage that came from her mouth. You could be miserable and rich just as easy as you could be miserable and poor? No one should be wowed by that line. I didn't realize she was shilling misery along with fool's gold."

Georgie swats me up and down the entire right side of my arm. "Would you hush? You're liable to get us booted right out of here."

"Georgie, I run the inn. No one is booting me out of..." I'm about to finish making my point when I spot a sight that makes my heart stop cold.

Jasper is locked in what seems to be a rather cozy conversation with Camila Ryder, his ex-girlfriend who looks as if she should be walking a runway in Milan, not at some slimy seminar on how to snag a man. She obviously doesn't need help in that department. A woman as gorgeous as Camila could snag any man she wants.

And then it hits me. I bet she found out that Jasper was staying here. Of course. It makes perfect sense. She didn't come here to listen to tips on how to snag a man. She came here to execute the plan—by stealing my man.

Jasper glances my way and does a double take once he spots me ogling them.

I turn away quickly and pop a pumpkin spice mini muffin into my mouth.

Great. He's going to think I'm spying on him. Worse yet, judging him for wanting to talk to someone that he's clearly intimately acquainted with.

Georgie leans in. "He's headed this way, Bizzy. And he's bringing a leggy brunette with him. What were you thinking bringing a sexy vampire like Jasper to this cesspool of wanting and desire? A dozen different women are bound to have their fangs sunk into him by the end of the night." She glances back and shudders. "Incoming. I'll be back." She scuttles off just as Jasper steps up with his old plus one.

"Bizzy"—Jasper's pale gray eyes seem to be pleading with me on some level despite the tight smile on his face—"I'd like you to meet an old friend. This is Camila Ryder. Camila, this is Bizzy Baker. She's the manager here at the inn."

Manager at the inn? Is that all I am?

I blink back at the cordial yet cold introductions.

Although, what was I expecting him to say? This is the love of my life?

We've just exchanged a few heated kisses. My heart sinks despite the fact. A part of me was hoping he would have given me a warmer title. Camila here gets to be his friend, while I'm the manager.

"So nice to meet you," I say. "Will you be needing a room at the inn?" I blink in disbelief that I even threw out the offer. Of course she doesn't need a room at the inn. She lives a hop and a skip away in Sheffield. Jasper told me as much just a few weeks back. And she happens to be the very reason he left that town.

Her mouth rounds out. "Actually, I would love a room. I'm

having my kitchen renovated. They just did the demo work yesterday and it's completely useless to me." Her lips curl my way. "What a great idea, Bizzy. And to think I thought I was doomed to a month of making coffee in the bathroom." A warm laugh bubbles from her, and I can't help but like her at least a teeny bit.

Me and my big ideas.

"What brings you to the seminar?" I clamp my lips shut tight because obviously I need a muzzle around the woman. I can't help it, though. She's so pretty and fun to be around. A ridiculous part of me wants her to like me.

She bats her long lashes at Jasper. "Leo and I are over." She shrugs. "Sometimes I do things that I really regret—and spending time with Leo Granger was one of them."

Perfect. It takes everything in me not to openly frown.

I remember Leo Granger. He showed up at the café last month, prying into my mind, letting me know that he could read them, too. I still cringe at the thought. He threatened to come back and hunt me down for who knows what.

Last month, at the Harvest at the Cove event, his aunt ran into Georgie, and Georgie inadvertently spilled the supernatural beans regarding the fact I can read minds. Word got back to Leo and he was immediately on the hunt. Needless to say, he tracked me down in record time.

Jasper's chest widens. *And here we go. Done with Leo, huh? I don't care to know the details.* His lips contort just this side of a frown.

Great. That must mean Jasper isn't interested in picking up where they left off.

Jasper nods. "I figured you woke up." Woke up? "Leo applied for the Seaview Sherriff's Department. Rumor has it, he got the position, too."

Camila chortles as if it were hilarious. "It seems all my exes head to Seaview." She looks my way. "Be sure to book me in a room near Jasper's. We've always been close." She bats her lashes up at him. *And I predict we're about to get a whole lot closer.*

I swallow hard. I don't wait for Jasper to reply, or Heaven forbid have a single positive thought about the two of them getting back together. Instead, I nod over at her.

"I'll get on that right away." I shoot Jasper a look without meaning to. "Excuse me." I head off into the crowd, embarrassed and enraged that I could be so ridiculous. If she wasn't already making inroads with Jasper, I sure as heck assisted.

I bump into a body, a man with dirty blond hair and a determined look on his face.

"Sorry," he says as he threads his way past me and pulls Shelby Harris to the side.

I bet he's with that organization of men Ginger threatened us with. I glance up, and sure enough Carter O'Riley and the boy brigade stride into the room. Not that I know which one is Carter, but I do know a herd of decent-looking men when I see them.

Here's hoping Camila spots one or ten she's far more interested in than she is Jasper. But that nagging feeling in my gut tells me that won't be happening. Face it, I'm not that lucky. And I've never been lucky in love. And with Camila on the opposing team? I don't stand a chance.

I'm about to head for the kitchen when Nessa heads straight for me, snaps me up by the hand, and soon we're sailing toward the front of the room with me trailing behind her like a kite.

"Bizzy, please tell my friends that I am simply working at the inn while I wait for some very important endeavors to fall into place for me."

Not this again.

Both Nessa and Grady are convinced their stint here at the inn is something beneath them.

Shelby Harris, the girl with an open face and strawberry blonde hair, shoots a look to her blonde counterpart, Chelsea. If I remember correctly, they have some influencer superpowers that have cast a spell over the world.

The copper-haired girl who walked in with them strides up. "Please, Nessa. You don't owe anyone an explanation of what you're doing with your life." She shoots both Shelby and Chelsea with death rays. "In fact, if I were you, I'd stay away from toxic people lest they drown you with their good intentions."

Shelby gags. "Nobody drowned you, Scout. You sank on your own. Besides, you're doing PR now for Ginger. You should be penning us a thank you note."

The blond man with the determined look on his face plucks Shelby by the elbow.

"Shel, please, this will only take a second."

"Don't you touch me, Luke." She yanks her elbow back and elicits a gasp among us.

A dark-haired man enters our midst, tall and strapping. His eyes glow like green orbs, and I could swear I just heard a collective sigh break out around him.

"Shel." He nods her way. "Chelsea." He offers the two of them amicable smiles before turning to the rest of the women who seem to be hypnotized by him. "I'm Carter O'Riley. If you're wondering where all the healthy, wealthy, and wise men are, they're currently at the refreshment table. I hear the muffins are to die for."

Shelby shoots him a look that could kill. "And here's another one that can thank me for the best career move he's ever made." *And to think he's begged to have me back every day since I walked away. Teaches him to cheat on me.*

"You've got a face that could launch a thousand ships, babe," Carter says it sweetly, and there's a tenderness in his eyes that lets me know he means it. *You've still got my heart, Shel. Please, just give me a minute of your time,* he pleads silently, and it's hard to listen to—even if I am prying into his mind to hear it.

Nessa scoffs. "More like the face that could sink a thousand mortgages. I've never been sorrier that I've ever met anyone before. If you're done with your dog and pony show, I'd like to ask you to leave now."

"Nessa!" I practically jump back, affronted that she's speaking to a guest that way. It's clear we'll have to revisit every golden rule of hospitality. I'm sorry that she doesn't care for the girl, but she's going to have to shelve it. Lord knows I've done it a dozen times myself whenever Mack shows her queen of mean face—and with Jasper hanging around, she seems to do it twice as often. Now there's one boyfriend of mine she won't get to steal—Camila just might beat her to it first.

Chelsea steps in, her eyes wide as a vicious smile expands over her face. "Yes, Nessa. Get back to the front desk where you're needed for important things like pointing people to the restroom."

Both Chelsea and Shelby indulge in a robust laugh, and Nessa looks as if she's ready to strangle them both.

"Oh, come on." Shelby waves Nessa off. "You're being ridiculous. And I'm certainly not talking mortgages with you. It's not my fault your father got in over his head."

Her father?

Nessa's face turns red as a pomegranate. "And no thanks to people like my father, *your* family is living high on the hog. You don't care. You're heartless, Shelby. Oh, I could just kill you." Nessa stalks off just as the blond man tries to pluck Shelby to the side once again, but Shelby snatches back her wrist as she growls at him.

"And I could just kill *you*," Shelby riots in his face before storming out of the ballroom herself.

I'm about to do the same when Ginger heads this way. "Where did Shel go?" she snips, that faux plastered smile finally dissipating from her face. "I can't hold this ugly mutt another second."

"Ugly mutt?" I balk at how brazenly rotten she's being. "He's adorable. Here, let me take him." I hold out my arms and she practically tosses the sweet angel at me. I drop a quick kiss over the pudgy little pooch's head and press his warm body to mine.

Ginger grunts, "I'd better wash up. He slobbered all over me. My goodness, I probably have rabies." She takes off and I can't help but scoff at her.

"How could she say those things about this precious little dumpling?" I sink another kiss right between his ears and his soft fur tickles my nose.

"Easy." Chelsea smirks. "She doesn't want anything to do with pets or babies." She shoots Scout a disparaging look. "Ginger's PR girl gave her brilliant advice and told her to steal a pet and pretend it's hers."

Scout straightens. "It *was* brilliant. That woman needs all the help she can to make her more likeable. She's a walking, talking nightmare. I didn't realize she would ask to borrow Shelby's poor puppy."

Chelsea glowers at the rear exit. "I better find Shelby." *But that dog will be the last thing we talk about.* She takes off for the rear of the room like a woman on a mission.

Scout smirks in her wake. "Good luck with that," she shouts in her wake. *She won't talk to Shel if I find her first.* She takes off into the crowd as music filters through the speakers and the din of conversations picks up a notch in octave.

I try to pry into the sweet pooch's mind, but he's practically shivering right out of his skin.

"I'd better get you somewhere quiet," I whisper to him as I head toward the door, but before I get there, I spot Jasper with a whole new, tall, beautiful brunette stapled to his side. Mack Woods.

And there she is. Boy, Mack never misses a boyfriend beat.

Just what I needed. A little competition for Camila. My heart sinks at the prospect of losing Jasper to either one of them.

A part of me is beginning to wonder if this relationship has been one-sided all along.

But I'm not sticking around to find out. Instead, I speed out the door and head right out of the ballroom where it's dead silent compared to the boisterous crowd roaring to life in there. An explosive rattle goes off and I stop dead in my tracks. Hopefully, that refreshment table didn't collapse on itself. I take a quick peek back inside, but everything looks as if it survived. I have a feeling that with this crowd that won't be the last explosive sound I'll hear tonight.

I pull Peanut up and drop a warm kiss to his forehead. "If you don't mind, I'm going to drop you off at the Critter Corner daycare. It's still staffed for another couple of hours, and I'll make sure to tell Shelby where to find you. I promise you'll be safe and comfortable."

The tiny ball of fur shivers in my arms. *Thank you.*

"Hey?" I give him a playful jostle. "You're welcome. I can hear your thoughts, by the way. Don't you listen to a thing that mean woman said. You're beautiful and sweet, and you don't have rabies."

He lets out a yelp that mimics a laugh. *You can hear me! And you're right. She is mean. A mean witch. I'd give anything not to be held by her again. Next time I think I'll resort to biting.*

"I wouldn't sink to her level. I'll talk to Shelby for you and see what I can do."

I'd appreciate that.

I speed us down a lone hall that leads to the rear of the building and note the back door is opened.

Odd. It's a staff only exit that leads to a dark courtyard. I've been meaning to string some lights up around there to give it a cozy appeal, but if anyone heads out there now they'll be met with a cobbled pathway that leads to Critter Corner and the forest that butts up to it.

Outside, the autumn sky is dark, save for a burnt orange glow signifying a spectacular sunset that just settled. The air is crisp and the maples are already shedding their papery leaves to the ground in colors of red and orange. There is no prettier sight than fall in Cider Cove.

An owl coos from high in the evergreens. A coyote howls into the night, and a mean shiver rides through me once again. It's as if something evil has descended on Cider Cove this October, and I shake my head at the thought.

Halloween will be here in just a few weeks, and that spooky night always gets the darker half of my imagination going.

I'm about to head to Critter Corner when I spot something along the cobbled path and I take a quick step back, holding onto Peanut tightly.

"Oh my goodness."

Lying on the ground with a bloom of crimson over her chest is Shelby Harris.

It looks like I won't be telling her a thing about Peanut.

Shelby Harris is dead.

CHAPTER 3

A knife-sharp scream evicts from me, so bloodcurdling, poor Peanut howls right along with me.

"*Shelby,*" her name rips from me so riotously loud my bones vibrate from the effort.

Not my Shelby. Peanut howls all the louder. **Shelby! Come back to me!**

In what feels like a blur, footsteps quicken from behind and a dark-haired man runs up panting. It takes a moment for it to register that it's Carter O'Riley.

"What's happened?" he barks it out with a marked aggression, and it takes everything in me to point to the ground. Lying on the cobbled path with her limbs splayed over red and yellow foliage is Shelby Harris, her eyes still opened to the navy sky above.

"Shelby!" Carter falls over her, doing his best to shake her to life as a barrage of footsteps hustle this way.

A pair of strong arms grips me from behind.

"Bizzy?" Jasper pulls me in momentarily, the stubble of his cheek brushing roughly over my face. "My goodness, are you okay?"

"Yes." And before I can say another word, Jasper is on the

29

ground checking Shelby's vitals, shouting at someone on his phone. A crowd blooms around us in a moment's notice, and Jasper bellows for everyone to take a step back.

"This is a crime scene." His silver eyes meet with mine. "There's been a homicide."

A gasp circles the crowd, followed by a series of screams.

Nessa runs up looking frazzled, her hair wild, her shirt slightly askew.

"Oh my goodness. Who did this?" She looks into the crowd with wide eyes, the look of fear streaming from her as if it were palpable. *My goodness, she's dead. She's really dead.*

A swarm of sheriff's deputies arrive, and soon enough they cordon off the area with caution tape that glows as bright as the sun. Chaos ensues as the crowd thickens. It's as if the entire state of Maine has flocked into the vicinity.

"Bizzy!" Georgie runs up and locks both poor Peanut and me in a crushing embrace. "Tell me you didn't do it. You killed Jasper's ex, didn't you?"

"Georgie," I say, plucking her off me. "Please, get to your cottage. It's too chaotic for you to be here—for anyone to be here."

"What am I supposed to do in my cottage with a killer on the loose?"

"I don't know. Break glass or something. We might need all the shards we can get to protect ourselves."

"Good thinking!" She's about to take off just as that blonde man who was trying to get Shelby to speak to him rushes the scene and bursts right through the barrier.

"*Shelby,*" he riots as he blasts through a couple of deputies, but before he can get to poor Shelby, a trio of men wrestles him to the ground.

Macy runs up and threads her arm through mine. "Bizzy, what just happened?"

Mom appears next to her, looking as if she were about to jump out of her skin.

"I don't know what happened," I say, glancing up at the worried faces surrounding me. "Look, I'm going to need your help wrangling everyone away from the area. Macy, why don't you and Mom usher everyone back inside?" I turn to Georgie. "I'm going to give you Peanut. Do me a favor—find Fish and take them both back to my place. This poor thing hasn't stopped shaking." I pull his furry face close to mine. "Don't you worry. I'll be back soon enough. You'll be safe. I promise."

Bizzy—his large brown eyes bulge my way—*I won't go with that woman. I won't go with Ginger. You can't make me.*

"I wouldn't dream of it," I say, pressing a quick kiss to his nose and handing him off to Georgie.

In less than a minute, my iron-handed mother and wonderfully bossy sister exert their superior powers of persuasion and the crowd quickly drains back inside the inn.

I turn to head toward the gaggle of deputies when I spot Jasper being accosted by Mayor Woods, and I can't help but glower at her. Mack clearly knows no bounds.

Jasper looks my way and squints before glowering himself. He's been known to be ornery, but there's something about that look I can't quite put my finger on.

I'm about to duck past the caution tape and put an end to Mack's barbarism when a hand falls softly over my shoulder, and I turn to find the real reason for Jasper's disdain. A tall deputy with dark, wavy hair and eyes laced with mystery and cockiness forces a smile my way.

"Bizzy." He nods. "Leo Granger. We met a few weeks ago in the café."

"I remember." I try my hardest to put my mind on lockdown. It was Leo, here, who all but accused me of reading minds.

Bizzy, I have a feeling you can hear me. His eyes search both of mine with a fiery intensity. *It's okay. I share your gift. There are others like us, too.*

"Others?" My fingers slap over my mouth and I turn to dash anywhere but here and end up smacking right into an all too familiar rock hard chest.

"What's going on?" Jasper grunts it out as he does his best to stare Leo down. "If you have anything at all that concerns this case, you come to me." Jasper blows out a breath before redirecting his attention my way. He pulls me in, those steely eyes bearing hard into mine. "Bizzy, I've got the inn on lockdown." His voice softens as he searches my features. "Why don't you get inside and make sure the guests are okay? The poor girl was shot. That means there's a gunman on the loose. I'll handle things out here." His eyes flash to Leo. *I'll make sure Leo steers clear. Just because he's got a beef with me doesn't mean it's open season on Bizzy. She's off limits and I'll make sure he knows it.*

Every last bit of me warms just hearing the quasi-threat.

Leo lifts a brow. *Someone is feeling insecure.* He tips his head my way. *I'm guessing he doesn't know about your neat little party trick.* His expression sours. *Only it's not a party trick, is it?*

I shake my head at him. "I'll gladly get inside, Jasper."

No sooner do I step away than Camila Ryder shoots out of the inn and into our midst like a missile. Her flowy long hair seems to have taken a life of its own as it sails behind her as if she were being chased by a dark cloud.

"Leo? Jasper?" she pants out their names. "Is it true? Is it Shelby?"

I take a step back. "Did you know her?" My adrenaline surges because a very small shallow part of me would love to pin her with the crime.

She nods while attempting to catch her breath. "I knew her. A little too well." *And as horrible as it is to admit, I'm not all that sorry she's gone.*

My mouth falls open as Leo and I exchange a quick glance.

I clear my throat. "Can I ask how you knew her?"

"Oh"—she shudders as a crisp breeze whistles by—"I don't remember. It's been a long time." She looks to Leo. *Some secrets are better dead and buried. Isn't that right, sweetheart?* "I'd better get inside." Her gaze hooks to Jasper. "It was really nice seeing you again. I'd say you were the highlight of my evening." She glances over to where the coroner's office is taking pictures of the crime scene. *The highlight of my evening until right about now.*

She offers a sly smile before speeding back into the small crowd still lingering behind us.

My heart thumps wildly at the strange exchange.

Someone calls for Jasper from the thick of the crime scene and he gently pulls me into his arms.

"Bizzy, please get inside." He flexes a sorrowful smile while warming my arms with his hands. "You're shivering. I'll be out most of the night, but I'm posting deputies all over the inn and the cottages—and I'm stationing one right in front of yours." His brows narrow over his pale eyes and it's a vexingly handsome look. "Bizzy, did you see anything suspicious at all when you came out here?"

"No, nothing. Not until I practically tripped over her body." I glance to the left and note the blond man—I think his name was Luke, staring sternly at Shelby's splayed out limbs.

Jasper glances over and nods. "I know what you're thinking, Bizzy. But promise me you'll leave this one to me. I'll catch the killer. You keep safe."

"Absolutely. My top priority is the inn. You have my word."

"Good." He sinks a kiss to my cheek. "Be careful." Jasper takes off and I spot Nessa heading over to speak to Luke, so I migrate that way as well.

Luke shakes his head at her as if they were having an unspoken conversation.

"Everything okay?" I ask, even though clearly everything is not anywhere near okay.

"Yeah." Luke takes a full breath, causing his chest to expand to the size of a door. "My girlfriend is dead. Everything is dandy." He says every word without taking his eyes off Nessa. Luke turns abruptly and ditches back into the crowd.

"What was that about?" I ask as we watch him leave.

"That was nothing." Nessa shudders. "Luke is a mess, that's all. And now so am I. I can't believe this is happening." *It's all a mess. A horrible, horrible mess. Of all people to die tonight, it's Shelby.*

I tilt my head over to her. "I know you didn't get along with Shelby. That must make this even harder for you in a way now that there won't be time to mend fences."

She pushes out a dull smile. "We weren't going to be mending fences anytime soon. And I feel terrible about it, too." She covers her mouth as she looks to the crime scene and we watch as the coroner covers Shelby with a glowing white sheet. "This is all my fault. She never would have died if it wasn't for me." Nessa bursts into tears before taking off for the inn.

"Nessa, wait!" I call after her as a trio of girls appears in her place. I recognize them from earlier in the evening. Chelsea—essentially Shelby's sidekick—

Scout—the girl Nessa said Chelsea and Shelby brought to ruin —and Ginger King herself.

Chelsea balks as if she just witnessed something incredulous. "Nessa just confessed." She barks it out so loud the murmur of the crowd grows quiet around her.

Ginger nods. "I heard her." She raises her voice an octave as she shouts the words toward the deputies standing a few feet away. "She says Shelby wouldn't have died without her. I think we've had a confession!"

A few of the deputies glance around as if wondering if they should take her seriously before heading this way.

Great.

"No." I shake my head. "That's not what she meant," I say, trying my hardest to come up with a reason why she didn't mean it that way. "She's tired. She's in shock, that's all. Nessa Crosby didn't kill anyone."

Scout slips a lock of her copper hair behind her ear as she looks hypnotically toward the commotion at the crime scene. "Somebody did this. Somebody killed Shelby." She looks to Ginger. "You're awful quick to point the finger at Nessa, aren't you?" Her lips flicker with the hint of a smile. "My word, you're not even crying."

Ginger shudders. "I don't do tears. My eyelash glue isn't that strong. I didn't cry at my aunt's funeral a few months back. I've practically trained myself to cry on the inside." She sniffs the air. "Like I'm doing now." *The heck I am. Goodnight, Shelby. Don't let the bedbugs bite—or should I say worms.* She glares at that white sheet sprawled over the ground as if she had a vendetta against it —or perhaps the poor body lying beneath it. She closes her eyes a moment and her chest rises as she takes a deep breath. *I'm safe. So safe. It's all over. It's all over now for good.*

She staggers back to the inn and my lips part in disbelief.

Chelsea steps over as far as the caution tape will allow.

My Shelby. My goodness, how did this happen? How did we ever get to such a dark place?

I watch as she follows Ginger and they melt back into the crowd.

I look at Scout with a great intensity as I struggle to read her mind, but I can't hear anything. She's nodding to herself, and her lips are twitching. Both are good indicators that she's locked in thought, but I can't get a read on it.

She turns to go and I quickly block her path.

"You're in charge of Ginger's PR, right?" I swallow hard, trying to think of why I might be asking—other than trying to break that strong as steel barricade she has around her thoughts.

"Yes." She gives a hard blink as if trying to wake up. "Don't worry about the seminar. It was all but over."

"I'd like to invite her to do another. That is, if she's up for it."

How crass to even think of such a thing—and at the crime scene no less. But the poor girl lying on the ground does deserve some justice, and I have a feeling the killer is still very much in our midst.

"I don't know what Ginger will or won't want to do." She shoots a quick look to where Shelby lies. "Maybe we can do a mixer. A Halloween theme? Ginger and Carter are always looking to throw their desperados together." She averts her eyes as if she wasn't buying any of it.

"Perfect. I have every weekend open this month."

She nods. "I'll get back to you." Scout gives one last glance Shelby's way and her lips flicker with the idea of a smile once again. "Goodnight," she says and a shiver runs up my spine as I watch her stride coolly back into the crowd.

My eyes search the area for clues as the wind picks up with an artic breeze. The sky darkens, save for a thumbnail moon, and the stars glitter over Cider Cove like crushed onyx diamonds.

I pick up on snatches of errant thoughts and I open my own mind in an effort to catch them all.

Poor thing.

I can't imagine what her family will go through.

The voices are coming quickly and I try to filter through the minutia of thoughts, mostly regarding the chill in the air, the fact the murder has left them stunned.

Shelby Harris is gone for good.

I twitch my head in the direction that voice came from. Unless I'm standing right in front of them, it's near impossible to know if it came from a male or female.

I'm glad she's gone. You know what they say—two of us can keep a secret if one of us is dead.

My eyes widen as I glance to the left.

I did it, says another.

My heart thumps to life as it riots in my chest.

And I'm going to get away with murder.

CHAPTER 4

*I*f there is one thing about the people of Cider Cove, it's that we can appreciate the seasons and tend to celebrate them to a fault. It's the very next day after the unthinkable crime that took place at the Country Cottage Inn, and Georgie, Macy, and I have taken to the task of delivering platters full of pumpkin spice mini muffins to the Haunted Harvest Festival. It's Saturday, and the Montgomery's farm is the nexus of the community as the whole town gathers to kick off fall the only way Cider Cove knows how—with hayrides and pumpkin carving contests.

No sooner do I get into the thick of the crowd at the harvest festival with my arms laden down with enough pumpkin spice mini muffins to feed a small island nation than I bump into a body. It takes all the staggering and rather terrible ballerina moves I can muster to keep the treats in my arms from going airborne.

A sharp howl of a cry comes from the woman—the aforementioned body, as she accidentally sloshes her colorful blouse with a glass of something pink and fruity.

"Oh my goodness!" I cringe. "I'm so very sorry!"

"Would you watch where you're going?" she's quick to bark my way. She's beautiful—an older woman, about my mother's age. Dark, glossy hair and a highly chiseled bone structure.

"Let me help you." I step forward just as she does the same and I nearly sever her neck with the platter in my hand.

"Good Lord, it's as if you're aiming for me." Her glassy gray eyes burn with fury. "How about this? You see me coming—you go the other way. I'm not mingling with the masses just to have my head sliced off by some wayward baker." She takes off and I can't help but scoff.

"I'm no wayward baker," I say halfheartedly in her wake.

"*Yeah*," Georgie calls after her. "Bizzy just so happens to burn everything she even *thinks* about baking."

"Good one," I say as we bustle through the crowds on our way to the big tent labeled *Good Eats*.

"I'm so glad I live in a world where there are Octobers," Macy says while making a face as she struggles to set down a couple of platters of pumpkin spice mini muffins, and both Georgie and I do the same. The entire dessert station at the Haunted Harvest Festival is already brimming with delectable sweet treats. But I have a hunch the goodies from the Country Cottage Café will soon take center stage. Emmie's treats really are that delicious.

Macy slaps her hands together from the effort. "Whose quote was that, anyway?" she asks, working her silvery blonde hair into a pert little ponytail. Just beyond my sister are rows and rows of birch, maples, oaks, and liquid ambers, their branches filled with fall's fiery glow as they rain down leaves in every citrine color.

"*Gandhi*," Georgie offers and I can't help but laugh.

"It was Lucy Maude Montgomery," I say. "And it's a famous quote from *Anne of Green Gables*. I loved that book." I shake my head wistfully as I glance around the crowds already brimming at the festival.

There's a huge orange and black banner strung up over the dessert station that reads *Happy Falloween!* And spread across the festival grounds are rides and games, jump houses for the little kids, hayrides for just about everyone, a cider press, a haunted maze, face painting, and a crafts station, too.

The Haunted Harvest Festival has long been touted as one of Cider Cove's premier events, and every year the Montgomerys try to outdo themselves by making the month-long event bigger and better—and both cozier and spookier all at the very same time. The Montgomerys' acreage is laden with groves and orchards of every variety. They grow everything you can think of from berries to beets, but during this month all attention goes to their much-adored pumpkin patch.

"Hey ho, the gang's all here!" a cheery male voice calls from behind and we turn to find my father looking handsome in a black dress shirt and jeans. A pair of black and white snakeskin boots adorns his feet and he looks dapper as usual. I got both my dark hair and icy blue eyes from that wily man. He's wearing his perennial sly grin, which only accentuates his slight comma-like dimples, and there's a general adorableness about him that has always served him well. I've yet to meet a soul who doesn't like my father. Even my mother *and* all my father's other handful of ex-wives still think he's a charming devil, emphasis on the afore-mentioned nefarious entity.

"Daddy!" Macy is the first to offer him a rather caustic hug. My sister has always worked ardently to be a daddy's girl. But thankfully, my father openly confesses to anyone he meets that he has two.

He quickly offers both Georgie and me a double embrace, and I inhale his familiar spiced cologne.

"So, what are you girls up to?" Dad's brows dip playfully as he tries his best to scowl. "I'm sensing trouble."

"No trouble," I'm quick to say. "Macy was showing off her literary prowess and gifting us with quotes that have to do with fall."

"*Ah.*" Dad lifts a finger in the air. "Let me guess. It was a classic. Life starts all over again in the fall."

Georgie moans and swoons, her eyes quickly growing watery as she bats her lashes at him. "A man who quotes F. Scott Fitzgerald has the power to rule my heart. But it wasn't that." She deadpans that last sentence before popping a pumpkin spice mini muffin into her mouth.

Georgie waves her hand wildly as if she could hardly swallow fast enough to get her next thought out. Her gray mane is somewhat tempered in a loose braid with just enough wiry stragglers loose to give off that mad scientist vibe that I sometimes think she aspires for. The kaftan she's donned for today's festivities is orange and yellow with gold threading woven throughout.

It always warms my heart to see that Georgie chooses her wardrobe to adhere to the theme in the world around her. Unlike my own red and black buffalo flannel, dark jeans, and brown suede boots. I've always believed in dressing for comfort. Although, I will admit that as soon as Jasper swirled through my mind, I cinched my flannel in a knot high around my waist in an effort to show off my curves.

"I've got to make tracks." Georgie plucks at the enormous yet empty tote bag over her shoulder. "The more people at these events, the more bottles. And judging by all the food trucks and snack shacks, I'm going to hit the glass motherload. I've already determined that the mural the city council has commissioned me to do will be made from one hundred percent repurposed glass. No cheating!" She wags a finger at us as if we were about to commit a recycling offense.

Macy offers a tight smile, a sure sign that my spicy sister is about to commission her sarcastic superpowers. "That's right, Georgie. Stick it to the man anyway you can."

Wish I could stick it to a man. My sister scours the crowd as if she were looking for a victim right about now. I know for a fact

Macy is both lonely and on the prowl. A lethal combination if ever there was one.

Georgie spikes a crooked finger in the air as she takes off. "I fully intend to stick it to the man!"

Dad shakes his head, that perma-smile of his never leaving his face. "And on that note, I think I'd better go off and do something for the environment as well."

"You?" Macy blinks back with surprise.

My father isn't exactly known as an environmentalist. He worked in financial management for most of his life, something he still dabbles in on the side. But he's mostly retired.

"Yes, me." Dad straightens as he surveys the crowd before us. "I've got to mine this place for lonely looking women." *Before I get too lonely myself.* He gives a quick wink as he takes off into the thicket of bodies.

Macy groans, "Get ready to meet wife number thirty. Speaking of his wives, I'm texting Mom to see if she's here with her new beau. Ten bucks says he's got more hair in his ears than he does on his head—he's probably got a wart on the tip of his nose, too."

I scoff over at my sister.

"What?" She shrugs. "It's almost Halloween. I'm getting into the spirit of things."

"The *evil* spirit." No sooner do I say it than I hear the faint call of my name, and I look up to see Nessa speeding this way with two friendly pooches on leashes as they walk quickly by her side. "Well, if it isn't the handsome Sherlock Bones and our new little friend, Peanut. Hello, boys! Glad you could make it," I say, bending over to give Sherlock a quick squeeze and a kiss before picking up Peanut.

Sherlock tips his head over at me. *Bizzy, this poor dog is wracked with grief. And he's fearful he'll have to live with a witch named Ginger. If there's anything that can cheer him up, we need to do it—and fast. He did have nice things to say about Fish. Apparently, the cantankerous kitty was kind to him in the night.*

Sherlock Bones is a red and white freckled mixed breed about medium build with the tenacity of a bear, the loyalty of a best friend, and a heart of gold. He's Jasper's best friend, and over the last month that I've come to know them, it's safe to say they've both won me over.

"Oh, Peanut," I say as I drop a kiss on his tiny brown nose. Peanut has an adorable white line that runs down his face and meanders down one cheek. There's a general sweetness about him that can't be denied, and true to what Sherlock says, he genuinely looks as if he's grieving. "I'm so sorry you're sad. But you're safe. And I promise, I won't let a thing happen to you." And by *thing* I mean Ginger.

Nessa gives a pitiful laugh as she scratches the cute babe between the ears. "He cried all the way over. I think you're right. Getting him out of the cottage was the best thing for him today. Fish really wanted to come, too, and she followed me all the way out to the main road."

"Thankfully, Fish knows better than to leave the cottage grounds. But there are far too many people here today for a cute little beast who refuses to be leashed."

Nessa shrugs. "I agree."

"How are you doing?" I lean her way. "Any whisperings in your social circle on who could have killed poor Shelby?" Peanut flinches in my arms and I feel terrible letting the words leave my lips. "I mean, assuming it wasn't random." And judging by the chaos around her that night, I don't think it was.

Any trace of a smile leaves Nessa's face. "I don't have any idea." She gives a dark look to something or someone in the crowd. "I'll catch up to you later, Bizzy."

She takes off before I can stop her, and just as she does, Macy threads her arm through mine.

"Mom called and said they're here," my sister grunts. "She says they're making out by the food trucks."

I glance to the sky with a laugh in my throat. "She did not say that."

"Okay, fine. She said it's time for her children to meet the old goat."

I know for a fact she didn't say that either. If Maximus Wilder looks anything like his brother, he's no old goat.

Macy navigates us to the rows and rows of food trucks to the one marked *Maximus* and my heart drums wildly at the prospect of meeting Jasper's brother for the very first time.

"There she is!" Macy squeals with delight as soon as we spot her and gives my arm the death squeeze. "Hey? Look at that hottie behind her," Macy moans in approval. "Wait a minute—isn't that your hottie?" She squints as we come upon Jasper's heart-stopping look-alike. But alas no, it's not my hottie. It's his brother. Technically, I haven't met any of Jasper's siblings, but I know for a fact he has three brothers and a sister. This particular brother's name is Maximus and he owns a restaurant in Seaview, which shares his same moniker.

Mom gasps once she sees us. Her hair is coifed and feathered circa 1983, and she's donned her preppy attire, stovepipe jeans, a coral cable knit sweater with a blouse underneath patterned with pumpkins. Her collar is popped with pride—the only way Ree Baker does it—and she looks amazing.

"You're here!" She glances back to Jasper's look-alike. "Max, you must meet my daughters." She leans our way with sudden death rays shooting out of her eyes. "Tell him my age and I'll disown you both before noon," she issues the threat lower than a whisper.

The six-foot-two, stunning wall of muscles steps over and wraps an arm around my mother in a spontaneous show of affection, and my sister all but falls to the ground.

A deep groan comes from Macy as if she were actually mortally wounded by the display of affection.

"Girls"—Mom brims with pride—"I'd like to introduce you to my new boyfriend."

"Mother?" Macy shakes her head in disbelief. "Please tell me this is his hot, *available* son and you couldn't wait to introduce me to him." She angles her head at the poor guy. "Anyone ever tell you that you look suspiciously like a detective from the Seaview Sherriff's Department?"

"Max Wilder." The six-foot wonder laughs as he extends his hand to Macy. "That would be my brother, Jasper, you're thinking about. And no, I'm not available." He winces. "I'm actually taken by this girl right here." He lands a tender kiss to Mom's cheek, and both Macy and I cringe—for two entirely different reasons.

Sherlock knocks his head to my knee. *Why is Jasper kissing your mother?* He jumps up quickly. *Oh, wait. It's his annoying brother. Proceed with caution. This one likes to scratch aggressively and tug at tails and ears.*

Something tells me my mother will enjoy all of the above, far too much.

Macy stares at Max's hand as if she didn't know what to do with it. I bet a part of her wants to smack him with it.

Macy shakes her head. *Maybe I should slap him with it? Maybe I should smack myself with it?*

A small laugh bubbles from me. "Bizzy Baker," I say as I shake his hand and position the sweet pooch in my arms better so they can see him. "And this is my new friend, Peanut."

Mom coos and scratches a finger over his head, and Max is quick to gift him a sturdy pat to the back.

"You're a Peanut, all right." Max chuckles. "Reminds me of one of my best friends growing up."

"You had dogs?" I ask.

"No, it was a kid down the street." He gives a little wink, and suddenly I'm starting to see a stark difference between him and Jasper. "And would you look at this?" He bends over and wrestles playfully a moment with Sherlock. "And if it isn't my favorite nephew. Hey? What are you doing here?" He gifts Sherlock a kiss on the forehead. "Don't tell me you've been dognapped." He looks up at me a moment. "Wait a minute." He straightens as a devious smile comes to his face. "You said your name is Bizzy Baker? You must be the girl at the inn my brother can't stop talking about."

My heart thumps at the thought. My heart seems to race at any thought of Jasper these days, but to think he's telling his family about me makes something in my spirit soar.

Max squints over at me. *Geez. Jasper wasn't kidding. She is beautiful. I can tell she gets her looks from this one.* He brushes a spontaneous kiss to Mom's cheek, and something about the action warms me. His mind certainly had the opportunity to wander in the wrong direction and it didn't. I think that says a lot about him.

Macy groans again, this time with her shoulders sagging as the reality sinks in.

"Nice to meet you, Max." She smacks her lips at our mother. "I definitely need a stiff drink. Or maybe one of those artisan pickles. How about both." She wanders off just as a girl who holds the same gray eyes and same dark hair as Max strides up with a hand lying protectively over her distended belly.

"Did I hear you say your name is Bizzy?" She smiles warmly. "I'm Ella Westbrook, Jasper's sister."

"The artist!" My eyes brighten her way. "Jasper told me you were having a showing this month."

"I sure am. And I want to invite your entire family to come out. It's free." She flicks her fingers at Peanut as if she were hungry to hold him. "Do you mind? I happen to have a soft spot for adorable tiny creatures."

Mom and I break out into a warm laugh as I hand Peanut over.

Bizzy, Peanut practically wails my name in fear. *Don't let her take me away. I'm quite comfortable with Fish and you.* He lets out a yelp and Sherlock chuckles to himself.

He wants me to bite her ankle. Sherlock nuzzles Ella's hip in a bid for her affection. *I'll do no such thing. She's got a pup of her own growing in her belly. My precious niece or nephew.*

Mom smiles over at her. "When are you due, Ella?"

"End of March, beginning of April. I'm rooting for March."

They share another laugh, but I'm stunted into silence. My mouth falls open with pure joy as I see my own six-foot-two stack of muscles walking over with a grin breaking out on his face, but before he can make his way over, Mayor Mack Man-Eater Woods is quick to accost him.

"Oh, thank goodness you're here." Mack presses a hand to her chest as if feigning distress. Mack Woods is never in distress. She *causes* distress to others—by way of pushing them into a whiskey barrel for example. I would be exhibit A. "There's a killer on the loose, and I just know a strong, intelligent man such as yourself will quickly apprehend them. I look forward to the public briefing. Maybe we could go for coffee afterwards? I'm sure Bizzy wouldn't mind if we spent some time together in the Cottage Café?" *And I'm sure she won't mind me helping myself to Jasper as well.* She shoots a cutthroat smile my way. *But then, you won't have a say in it. Will you, Bizzy?*

Mack has always been an expert at stealing what's mine— namely the men I'd like to keep for myself. I'll admit, a part of me is horrified at the thought of history repeating itself.

She stalks off in her high-heeled boots that a very shallow part of me admires and bright orange pea coat pulled tightly over her body. At least she'll be easy to spot in the crowd. And I will definitely be walking the other way.

Jasper shakes his head, his lips curving right back to a smile. "Bizzy Baker." He grins as he wraps his arms around me quickly. Jasper leans back and ushers an all too familiar older brunette into our midst, and I recognize her as the woman I ran into once I arrived. "This is one of your newest residents at the inn. Bizzy, I'd like to introduce you to Gwyneth Wilder, my mother."

I suck in a quick breath at the sight.

His mother's mouth rounds as her body grows visibly rigid. *Horror of horrors. It's the dimwit who tried to decapitate me. Heaven knows what she'll be capable of with my son. Let's hope this is nothing more than a flash in the pan—a rebound I think they call it.*

"Mom, meet Bizzy." Jasper takes a half-step back and I hesitate a moment before extending my hand.

"Pleasure to meet you, Gwyneth." I never said I was above lying. Granted, she's in a different environment, forced to move into an inn, and dealing with the crowds at the local pumpkin patch. I think I can let one errant comment slide.

Max steps in with my mother in tow. "And this is the woman I was telling you about. Mom, meet Ree Baker."

"Excuse me?" Gwyneth shakes her head. "What woman? The new night manager for the restaurant? Please Lord, let it be the new manager." *My son cannot be dating this relic from an era gone by.*

"*Mom.*" Max breaks out into a belly laugh. "This is the love of my life."

"Ree Baker?" She winces at the two of us. "Say it isn't so."

Mom gurgles a dark laugh.

One thing is for sure, Ree Baker isn't afraid to go toe-to-toe with anyone.

"Oh, it's so, Gwyneth." Mom curls her lips just shy of a smile. "And Bizzy is my daughter."

Kill me.

Gwyneth looks as green as a gourd.

"Bizzy?" someone shouts my name from behind, and I turn to find Nessa running this way. I quickly excuse myself to meet her.

"What is it?" I ask with Sherlock dancing between us.

47

"I have a confession to make." Her brows are furrowed, her lips quivering with fear.

"You're not going to confess to being the killer, are you?" I tease.

Her lips press tight. "Maybe I am."

CHAPTER 5

*A*utumn brings so much with it, an abundance of flaming red leaves, pumpkins dotting the landscape everywhere you look, and pumpkin spice treats that I look forward to all year long. And yet, this autumn brought something unexpected with it —something very much unwanted—*murder*.

Just as Nessa was about to fill me in on whatever it was that was stressing her out yesterday at the Haunted Harvest Festival, she caught a glimpse of Jasper and lost her nerve. She let me know in no explicit terms that she would confess everything to me as soon as she got to work tomorrow—which would be today. In fact, Nessa is due to work in just a few minutes.

The Country Cottage Inn is festooned for fall with silk maple leaf garland lining the counters and entry.

"What do you think?" Jordy nods for me to admire his handiwork at the entry to the inn.

Jordy, my best friend Emmie's brother, is the groundskeeper here at the inn. He shares Emmie's dark hair and bright blue eyes, and he just so happens to be my ex-husband. It's a long story not worth telling. We were in Las Vegas, got shnockered off Jim Beam, married, and had the marriage annulled before you could say happily *never* after. My brother, Huxley, happens to be a divorce attorney and he helped dissolve the brief matrimonial disaster.

I look up at the fall leaf garland, the spider webs strewn throughout, and the miniature orange twinkle lights and sigh.

"Jordy!" A laugh tickles my throat. "It's spectacular—and spooky. It's *spooktacular*."

"Glad you like it." He waves me over to the front doors. "Check out the front."

Both Sherlock and Peanut follow him as if they were as excited as I am to see it.

Sherlock twists his neck as if beckoning for me to hurry. **Looks good, Bizzy! When can I eat them?**

Peanut gives a playful growl at his new four-legged freckled friend. **Eat them and it will be your last day as a greeter at the inn.**

"You got that right," I whisper with a sly wink their way.

I step around the marble counter and both Peanut and Sherlock follow along. I usually only have Fish with me out on the prowl when I'm working the reception desk, but both Sherlock and Peanut asked to come along this morning. It was either that or they'd be relegated to Critter Corner in the back. And even though Critter Corner is more of a spa than a daycare, they still prefer it out front where all the action takes place—and to be honest, the guests do, too.

"Oh, Jordy, I love it," I say, admiring the thick ropes of maple garland trimming the enormous double door entry both inside and out. Tiny orange twinkle lights are woven throughout it and it gives off a haunted magical appeal. "Who knew you had a decorator's touch?"

"Not me—because I don't have one. Emmie told me to do it. She said she saw it online and she thought it'd be cute." He says cute as if it were a genuinely foul four-letter word. "I'm spending the rest of the day arranging that load of pumpkins the Montgomerys dropped off. Anything in particular you want me to do with them?"

"Line the cobbled path that leads to the entry for sure. Then stack some on either side of the doors. Oh, and make sure you put some on the periphery of the steps as you come on in. Of course, the café will need some—and outside of the café."

Jordy twitches his brows. "So basically everywhere." A warm chuckle expels from him. "Isn't it ironic? Here we were married for less than a day and yet you're still bossing me around with a honey-do list?"

A laugh bubbles from me. "That's because I am your boss."

The crisp fall breeze picks up and in walks Camila Ryder, a tall brunette with cut features and a knowing smirk on her face as she greets me with a smile. Her skin looks beautifully bronzed, and her lips are perfectly pouty and pink. Everything about her screams supermodel.

I bet if she never cheated on Jasper they would still be together. A part of me wonders if now that she's no longer with Leo Granger, mind reader extraordinaire, if Jasper wants her back. My stomach churns just thinking about it.

Sherlock moans and threads himself between my knees. *It's her again. It's that woman. She never shared her food with me, Bizzy. Not one time. Not one piece of bacon.*

I give a secret smile down at the disparaging pup. I happen to be notorious for sneaking him an extra slice of bacon.

Camila extends a hand my way. "Hello, Bizzy. I'm Jasper's friend. We met the other night." *Bet she's thrilled to see me.* She lifts a brow as if the thought amused her.

"Hi, Camila." I give her ice-cold fingers a shake. "Of course, I remember you." How could I forget? And *friend*? I guess she doesn't like the title of ex-girlfriend. "What can I do for you?"

Her lips purse, and suddenly it looks as if she's feigning a pout. "I'm actually ready for that room. The remodel on my kitchen just kicked into high gear and I'll be out for a month at least. Gwyneth, Jasper's mother, and I are very close." Her eyes rake over me as if she wanted that little not-so friendly tidbit to sink in a moment. "She mentioned she was stuck here, too. It'll be fun to join both her and Jasper—like one long sleepover." *And I will be sleeping with Jasper.* She glances down at Sherlock Bones and frowns. *Hopeful this beast won't be anywhere near the bedroom this time.*

Ugh. The things poor Sherlock was subjected to. I'd better give him an entire platter of bacon to make up for it.

Camila practically snarls at him for no good reason.

The way a person responds to animals says a lot about him or her, and right now it's not saying great things about Camila.

And did she say *stuck* here? She's more than welcome to get stuck anywhere between here and Sheffield.

I nod over to her. "I'm sure we have a room for you. In fact, I'll get you registered right away." A thought comes to me. "Camila? The other night you mentioned that you knew Shelby Harris. Was she a colleague of yours?" I happened to know they work in entirely different fields. Shelby lived the lifestyle of the rich and famous, and Camila is a high school guidance counselor.

She tips her head back and takes a deep breath. "I guess you could say so. We met when she came to the campus I work at. It was part of Career Week. She and her partner shared about their experiences as influencers." *And boy, do I regret ever being there.*

I swallow hard, trying to figure out how to best delicately pull the details from her.

"She mentioned you were good friends." I shrug, marveling at how easily the lie slipped from me.

Her eyes widen with horror. "What else did she say?" *I'll never forgive myself for giving in to her ridiculous ideas. Modeling—of all the cheesy ploys I fell for.* She averts her eyes.

I take a quick breath. "She mentioned something about pictures." I shake my head as if I couldn't quite recall—because I can't.

Camila's lips round out. "Oh, right. It was stupid. She had a photographer friend who needed someone for something. A quick job and I took it."

Jordy steps up, his eyes still glued to Camila's perfect features. *Geez, I didn't know they made them like this. Holy heck. Where do I sign up?*

Good Lord. At least he kept it G. I've accidentally intercepted a lot more colorful thoughts from Jordy where the opposite sex is involved.

"Camila, this is Jordy," I say. "He's our groundskeeper here at the inn."

Jordy clears his throat. "This is just an in-between job. I worked in upper management for years. I just needed a break."

She voluntarily shakes his hand. "Camila Ryder. I'm a high school counselor over in Sheffield." *My, aren't you a mighty fine snack.* Her smile widens as she examines him. *If I weren't throwing out the bait to net my ex, I'd hop on the Groundskeeper Express.*

Knew it! She is trying to *net* her ex!

I practically stop breathing at the thought. Which reminds me...

"Jordy, pull out those witches' hats. Those are fun to decorate with, too." I shoot Camila the side-eye. I'm sure they'll come in handy with the coven that's taking up residence at the inn.

Fish slaps the counter with her long fluffy tail as I arrive at the computer. *Bizzy, is that the girl you were telling me about? Camila?*

I nod over at my sweet cat. Having Fish living with me has been like having a best friend or a sister by my side twenty-four seven. And considering the fact that neither my siblings nor best friend knows anything about my ability to pry into other people's minds, Fish is closer to me than both.

Let me take a better look at her. Fish tips her head to the side as she examines the girl. *Sure she's pretty, but I can tell she's cunning, too. I don't like cunning. It brings out the worst in people.*

Peanut curls up in a ball of cuteness by my feet as I quickly assign Camila to a room.

"What do you know?" I say. "You'll be right next door to Gwyneth. A room just opened up. The room won't be ready for about twenty minutes, so you might want to head to the café out back. It sits right in front of the cove and has sweeping views of the Atlantic."

"Perfect." She types into her phone. "I just asked Gwyn to join me." She wrinkles her nose my way. "I'm sure once she gets to know you better, she'll invite you to call her Gwyn. All of her close friends do. Oh, and I spoke to Jasper. He'll be here in a few minutes. Would you be a love and tell him where to find me?" Her lips curve with a dangerous smile. "It's so nice that I'll be practically living with him and Gwyn. They've always been like family." She trots off in the direction of the café and I can't help but scowl at her.

She's not even hiding the fact she wants him back. And what does she mean, she just spoke to Jasper? Do exes speak to one another on the regular? Is that a thing?

Of course, I *work* with mine. But Jordy and I didn't date for four years only to have me cheat on him with his co-worker.

No sooner do I get the thought out than a sheriff's deputy enters the inn and gives a jovial pat to Sherlock's head.

"Hey, old buddy. I've missed you." The deputy straightens only to reveal himself as Leo Granger.

Well, there you go. Speak of the devil and he will come. Or in my case *think*. Same difference when the devil in question is a mind reader.

He winces as he heads my way. His wavy hair is combed back and his dark eyes are squinted with laughter as if he were in on some horrible joke. And sadly, he sort of is.

Devil? He shakes his head. *Now is that any way to talk about your fellow transmundane?*

Trans what? Now it's me shaking my head at him. I figure I've already outted myself to the deceptive deputy. There's no backing out now.

Sherlock runs over to my side of the counter. *Careful, Bizzy. He'll try to hypnotize you with his eyes. That's exactly how he stole Camila.*

I make a face at Leo for doing anything of the sort. Although, I should probably be penning him a thank you.

Leo barks out a laugh. "That you should. And do you prefer to talk?"

"Yes," I hiss. "But keep it down." Partly because I'm not so sure I should be talking to him in particular. "What's this *transmundane?*" I whisper.

He shrugs as he leans in. "That's what we are. I have an aunt that's just like us. The one that happened to lead me to you last month."

"Knew it." I strum my nails against the counter. Georgie somewhat outted me, and the woman ran with it at the craft festival. Mack put the event together, and I should have known anything that Mayor Woods touches would endanger me in some way.

Before I can ask another question, a sassy older brunette with stunning gray eyes that I've grown to have a slight obsession with —on her son, that is—pops up at the reception counter.

"Gwyneth, how can I help you?" I force a cheery grin, although that condescending smirk she's wearing lets me know I shouldn't be too thrilled to see her just yet. Her hair is wavy and shellacked into place. Her lips look hardened with a harsh shade of orange, and her mascara is clumping her lashes into groups of two and three.

Her smile tightens in my direction. "I'm meeting with Jasper's special friend in the café. As soon as he gets here, do redirect him. I'm trying so hard to get those two lovebirds back where they belong." Her head twitches toward Leo as if her sixth sense just alerted her to his presence. "Deputy Granger? Oh, Leo." She pulls him in for a quick embrace. "How ever are you doing? Don't answer that. I heard all about Camila breaking your heart. You know you can't have her. But there are plenty of fish in the sea." She sucks in a quick breath as she looks my way. "Come to think of it, you and *Dizzy* would make a fine pair. Why don't the two of you take a lunch break and get to know one another?" The whites of her eyes expand as she gives a quick chortle. "Of course, I'd like a special mention at your wedding for coming up with the idea. You'll both thank me in a year." She points a red fingernail at the two of us as if she were casting a spell before trotting off.

Sherlock whimpers and Peanut follows suit.

Is she gone? Sherlock trots out from behind the counter to get a look. ***Oh, thank heavens. And who is this Dizzy person, anyway?***

I shrug over at Leo. "She's my biggest fan. What can I say? Dizzy Baker at your service. Now, what is this transmundane business? You said that's what we're called. How do you know? How does your aunt know?"

He opens his mouth to answer just as Nessa speeds over and cranes her neck at him. Her face looks white as a sheet at the sight, and if I didn't know better, I'd say Nessa was most definitely acting like a killer who didn't want to be sent up the river for a very long time.

"On second thought, Detective Granger"—my voice spikes unnaturally—"why don't you inspect the grand ballroom one more time? I have absolutely no problem with that."

He takes off, but his eyes are slow to peel away from mine.

"Oh wow, he's hot, Bizzy," Nessa pants as she shoves her purse into the cabinet below the reception counter. Her dark hair is swept back into a bun and she's wearing a cinnamon-colored sweater made of spun yarn that looks feather soft and cozy. "Oh my goodness!" she coos as she picks up Peanut. "Hey there, sweet boy. Has anyone ever told you that you've got the face of an angel?" She presses a long, lingering kiss between his ears and Peanut's tubby little tail wags happily.

I like her, Bizzy! Peanut squeals out loud as he says it. *Can I keep her? Can I keep her?*

Fish yowls with laughter. *I think Peanut has found his person. He's in love.*

"I think Nessa is in love for sure," I say as I give Peanut a light scratch over his back. "So, what's going on?" I ask, examining her features, and that distressed look comes right back to her face.

"Oh, Bizzy. I've really done it this time." She falls back onto a stool and holds Peanut all that much tighter.

"What?" I pant with baited breath. "Tell me. It'll all work out, I'm sure."

"Not if I'm locked up behind bars forever." She presses her lips tight. "Bizzy, it's no secret that I didn't like Shelby. And do you know how she died?"

"She was shot." I nod. "I think everyone knows that by now."

"Yes, but do they know she was shot with my gun?"

"What?" I squawk so loud, Fish, Sherlock, and Peanut all jerk their heads my way. "Nessa, you don't have a gun, do you?"

She shrivels in her seat. "Okay, don't get mad. But after that murder last month, my dad made me go out and get a concealed carry permit. And, of course, he bought me a small handgun to go along with it—a .38 Special. I had lessons down at the shooting range and everything."

My mouth rounds out in horror. "My goodness, Nessa, did you kill Shelby Harris? Was it an accident?"

She shakes her head in disbelief, wisps of hair falling loose around her face.

"I keep my gun in my purse, right underneath the cabinet. When I got home that night, I went to put it away and opened the cylinder just to inspect it. My heart stopped once I saw a dimple on the primer in the back of the casing. It's a sure sign that the bullet has been spent. I pulled it out and took a closer look, and I was right." Her forehead breaks out into three deep-set worry lines. "Someone fired my gun, Bizzy. And it wasn't me."

I study her a moment, both my mind and hers reeling with panic.

Peanut suddenly begins to squirm. *She did it! She killed my Shelby. Help! Get me down! Killer on the loose. Killer on the loose!*

I take the anxious creature from her and dot him with a kiss before setting him on his feet.

"Nessa, how do you think the gun got from your purse to the killer?"

"I don't know. I mean, we both know Grady is prone to wander from the counter and take extended breaks for no reason. The reception counter could have been unmanned for hours. Anyone could have retrieved it." She cinches her eyes shut tight and holds her breath a moment. "Chelsea—Shelby's partner —Chelsea Ashley, she knew I have a permit to carry." She presses a hand to her chest. "That's right. She freaked out once she heard the seminar was at the inn. She swore it was probably haunted after what happened last month. She didn't want to come. I had to convince her it was safe. I even joked that I would be patrolling the grounds with my weapon. Of course, I wasn't. But she asked what I meant and I told her that my father bought me a gun. I'm sorry, Bizzy. I never meant to bring any trouble to the inn."

I try my best to process everything she's just spilled at my feet. "Do you think Chelsea had a motive to kill Shelby?"

Nessa glances back at the ballroom. "I don't know. I heard rumors about something." She brings her fingers to her mouth and takes a nip at her crimson-colored fingernails.

"What rumors? You can tell me, Nessa. I need to know."

She shrugs it off. "Something about a favor Chelsea did for Shelby. Chelsea told me that after the incident happened it almost split their friendship apart. But that she was glad it made them stronger. I won't lie. She didn't look happy about it. She looked downright angry. I don't know exactly what happened, but if Shelby was twice as shady as her father, it was very, very bad."

A shiver runs through me just as a dark figure walks through the front door, and a sense of relief washes over me in an instant.

Detective Jasper Wilder looks dressed to kill—pardon the pun—in a dark suit with a slick navy tie, his gun holster peeking from underneath his jacket. Jasper looks hot to trot, and if I had my way I'd trot him right over to my cottage.

"Hey, Bizzy. Hello, Nessa." He nods her way. Sherlock goes bonkers as he prances around Jasper, hungry for attention—and if it weren't for Nessa's news, I'd probably do the same.

I got the job! I got the job! Sherlock's tail wags like a whip as he hops up on his hind legs. *I'm the official greeter of the Country Cottage Inn! Fish and I are double teaming 'em.*

I can't help but bite down a smile. It's adorable to see Sherlock basking in his *greeter* glory.

"Jasper." I'm about to head around the counter when Nessa grabs me by the hand.

"Bizzy, we can't tell him." She pleads twice as hard with her eyes.

"Tell me what?" Jasper offers a crooked grin as he settles those intense gray eyes to mine and I melt like a marshmallow in a cup of hot cocoa.

Oh no. Nessa moans. *Bizzy is going to blabber it all to her new boyfriend, and I'm going to spend the rest of my life on a chain gang on I-95.*

I crimp my lips at her. "Nessa, you're innocent, aren't you? It wasn't you who pulled the trigger."

Her expression grows cold before she softens. "No, it wasn't." She looks to Jasper as her body stiffens. "I am one hundred percent innocent." *I'm sure they all say that in the big house. Isn't that the bridge of the prison choir?*

Jasper's playful demeanor quickly dissolves and in its place is that hard-boiled detective look that means business.

"What's going on?"

I look to Nessa and she closes her eyes and gives a slight nod.

In less than ten seconds, I relay everything Nessa just told me.

Jasper's eyes widen a notch. "Nessa, do you have the gun with you?"

Nessa sags a moment before retrieving her purse from underneath the counter.

"Take the whole thing," she says. "Maybe the killer left their prints on it."

I pull a paper bag from the shelf beneath me and Nessa drops her purse inside.

"I have my license in my phone case," she says. "And that's in my pocket. I don't need anything in there right now." She takes the bag from me and hands it to Jasper.

Jasper holds the bag to the side as if it were filled with death, and it just might be in the proverbial sense.

"I'll have forensics inspect it." He presses out a depleted smile. "They have the bullet that killed Shelby. We'll see if it matches your gun."

"How will they do that?" I ask out of morbid curiosity.

Jasper lends those gray eyes my way. "Bullets tend to have distinct indentations carved into them as they leave the chamber called lands and grooves. They'll have to fire a round of Nessa's gun to see if they match."

I nod. "It's like a fingerprint then?"

"Exactly."

"Jasper?" a male voice calls out from the right and we find Deputy Granger stepping into our midst, looking like the cat who swallowed the canary.

"What are you doing here?" Jasper grunts.

"Bizzy invited me to inspect the ballroom once again." Leo offers a cheesy grin without missing a beat.

Why do I get the feeling Leo enjoys tormenting Jasper and

he's using me to do it.

Jasper glances my way. "I'm not buying it. What are you really doing here?"

A tiny laugh begs to bubble from me at the thought of Jasper knowing me so well.

Leo shrugs. "You're the one who put in a request to roam the grounds. I'm simply working my detail for the day." His features harden. "Camila is having lunch with your mother in the café."

"Is she?" Jasper turns his head in that direction, and I can't help but frown at Leo.

What did you do that for? I snip.

Leo's lips expand, no smile—and he certainly doesn't say a word, verbally or otherwise. It's a strange trick not many people can pull off. Just the wicked ones seem to have mastered it, and I don't mind one bit if he heard that last part.

Jasper takes a breath, his chest expanding the size of a door. "Bizzy, I'm going to say hello to my mother. I'll be back in less than two minutes." He looks to poor Nessa, who's shivering like a lamb to the slaughter. "If you don't mind, I'd like to question you. It won't take long. I promise."

Nessa gives the hint of a nod.

I knew there would be trouble. She shakes her head as she looks out the opened doors. *I should run. Better yet, I should tell the whole truth. Lord knows I don't owe him any favors. If anything, he owes me.*

I glance to Leo a moment.

Who is she talking about? I ask mostly to myself. *Is she talking about Jasper?*

Leo shakes his head. *She's covering for someone.*

And I'm afraid he's right.

Jasper comes back and cinches a tight smile over his lips as if he were mildly guilty of something.

I don't bother smiling back. I'm betting Camila has cast her spell over him once again.

Jasper leans in. "I'm sorry about all the chaos. I'll make it up to you. I promise." He turns to Leo. "Why don't you head over to the café and join them? You don't have anything to discuss with anyone here." His eyes harden with a threat.

Okay, so I'm more than thrilled to have Jasper hovering protectively over me. And perhaps rightly so considering the fact Leo is infamous for swiping what isn't his. Although, that's the difference between Camila and me. I'm not going anywhere. I'm virtually unswipable.

Leo nods my way. "I'll see you later, Bizzy."

And we'll continue where we left off, I say.

He nods as he presses his gaze to mine. *Indeed we will.*

Leo takes off, and Jasper scoffs.

"See that? He's trying to make me think he's having some deep, meaningful moment with you. The guy is nuts. I'd steer clear if I were you." *It boils my blood to think of Leo trying to weasel his way into Bizzy's good graces. What the hell did I ever do to him, anyway?* He shakes his head. *He could have kept Camila forever. But he can't have Bizzy.*

He offers a meager smile. "Nessa? Why don't we head to the ballroom where we can get some privacy?"

Jasper leads the way with a happy Sherlock bouncing by his side, and Nessa reluctantly follows along as if he were taking her to the gallows.

Poor thing. Peanut whines and I pick him up. *She sure looks guilty, doesn't she?* He murmurs it out so Fish can hear.

Fish traipses over and rubs her head against my arm. *Oh dear, Bizzy. Our Nessa couldn't have done this and we both know it. But it sure looks like trouble.*

"It sure does," I say.

I think I'd better pay Chelsea Ashley a visit.

Trouble has come to the Country Cottage Inn once again.

Something tells me this October will be a real killer.

It's already proven to be just that.

CHAPTER 6

*a*utumn is ablaze in all its glory as Emmie, Sherlock, and I walk along the Montgomery's farm right after sunset.

It turns out, tracking down Chelsea Ashley was easier than I thought it would be. Apparently, leaving breadcrumbs to where she is at all times is a part of her job as a social media influencer. And that led me right back to the Haunted Harvest Festival at the pumpkin patch. There's not only a chill in the evening air, there's most definitely a *thrill* as townspeople young and old have poured onto the Montgomery's farm looking to soak in all that fall has to offer. The scent of cinnamon-spiced cider clings heavy in the air as the murmur from the thick crowd and the intermittent bouts of laughter explode all around us.

Sherlock howls as the sound of a horn goes off from a distance. **This is the place to be, Bizzy! Let go of the leash. I promise I'll behave. Just one quick lap around that pumpkin patch.** He stops short as we're about to pass the petting zoo. **Are those goats? Oh, let me see the goats, Bizzy. Let me see the goats!**

"Maybe later." I can't help but laugh. "Keep up, Sherlock. There's no way I want to lose you in this crowd. I don't think

Jasper will ever speak to me again if I come home shy of one Sherlock Bones."

Jasper hadn't come home from work yet, so I thought I'd bring Sherlock along on tonight's little investigative effort. Nessa volunteered to watch Peanut for me. And Fish was fast asleep as soon as I fed her that Fancy Beast cat food she lives for.

"I don't know, Bizzy." Emmie shakes her head as we navigate through the crowd with our arms laden down with platters full of pumpkin spice mini muffins. "I wouldn't want my boyfriend's ex taking up residence at the inn. That's just asking for trouble. I'll bet you every one of these muffins she's still after him."

"Oh, she is. She all but said so." She *thought* it—and I just so happened to intercept those delusions of grandeur. At least I hope they pan out to be nothing but delusions. "But I'm not too concerned."

My lips twitch, the way they're prone to do when I'm stretching the truth.

"You're not too concerned?" Emmie steps in front of me, causing me to nearly topple the trays in my hands.

Emmie looks adorable with her long oatmeal-colored duster and her ripped jeans with the holes in her knees. I've yet to jump on the holey trend, but I'm afraid I'll look more like a farmhand than I will anything adorable. On Emmie, even these stylish quasi-rags make her look as if she belongs on a runway. Come to think of it, with my orange and black plaid flannel and my well-worn jeans, I sort of do look as if I've spent far too much time on a farm.

She squints over at me. "Liar, liar, twitchy lips on fire. You're concerned, Bizzy. I've known you long enough to read you like a book. That girl is out to steal your man. She's got her claws and her high heels out. I saw the way she looked as we left the inn this evening. She was dressed to kill—your relationship. I'm telling you, Bizzy. Your relationship had better watch its back."

A tiny growl works its way up my throat. "I don't want to

think about it. Besides, Jasper is busy with a brand new homicide investigation. He doesn't have time for Camila's head games right now. She couldn't have picked a worse moment to try to pry her way back into his life."

Sherlock lets out a sharp bark. ***Don't worry, Bizzy. I'll fight tooth and nail to keep you.***

"Thank you," I mouth his way.

No sooner do Emmie and I put our sweet treats down at the dessert table than she elbows me in the ribs.

"There she is," Emmie whispers. "Suspect number one. Right over by the hot apple cider booth."

Both Emmie and I scoured over pictures of Chelsea before we left the inn. The name of Shelby and Chelsea's social media site is called S&C's Shenanigans. There was a big tribute to Shelby on the front page of their official website today. Chelsea asked her fans to bear with her while she takes some time to grieve. But at the moment, Chelsea isn't exactly grieving. She's busy taking pictures of herself sipping hot cider, and carefully arranging a group of tiny pumpkins on a bale of hay and taking artful pictures of them as well.

Emmie leans in. "There's a hottie in the crafts booth teaching the masses how to paint the insides of Mason jars. I'll go get crafty with the cutie. You go catch a killer, Bizzy. Find me when the dirty deed is done—unless, of course, I'm lucky enough to do a dirty deed myself."

"*Emmie.*" I laugh.

"What? Painting is messy work." She gives a cheeky wink. "Don't worry. You're still my ride home." She gifts Sherlock a quick pat to the head before taking off.

The moon hangs low against a deep purple sky while the stars spray out like crushed diamonds over Cider Cove tonight.

Everywhere you look there are cutouts of witches and ghosts adorning the booths and stands. Jack-o-lanterns glow, carved in every incantation that the spooky season has to offer, and some are painted with stripes, checkers, and polka dots. Miniature barrels brimming with mums in bright yellow, burnt orange, and deep maroon are strewn about the grounds. And families abound with pumpkins in their arms. Little boys and little girls run around screaming as the night curdles with their laughter.

There's even a mile long line to catch a ride on one of those haunted hayrides.

A part of me wishes Jasper were here to do exactly that with. In fact, I think I'll make it a point to have a date with him right here at the Haunted Harvest Festival. There's nothing more romantic than sipping cider in the fall with leaves crunching below your feet and a baby-faced moon overhead. Fall has a magic all its own, and right about now, I'm craving a little magic with my favorite homicide detective.

Sherlock jumps and barks. *We're getting close, aren't we, Bizzy? There's a killer nearby. I can feel it.*

"You can feel it?" I ask as I pull him close and give him a quick scratch between the ears. I've heard of dogs sensing earthquakes and helping detect diseases. If Sherlock could sniff out a killer, that would be quite the talent. "Try to be friendly," I whisper as we head her way.

Chelsea has her hair piled in a bun. She's wearing a scarlet cardigan that reaches her knees and keeps slipping off one shoulder as she struggles to get just the right shot of the pumpkins before her, and that's exactly when I decide to intercept her.

"Chelsea?" My voice comes out a touch too friendly. In truth, we don't even qualify as acquaintances.

The girl spins my way with her eyes widening the size of dinner plates. *I knew coming here was a mistake. People are going to think I'm a monster. Never mind the fact I sort of am.*

"Can I help you?" She blinks my way and her eye shadow glitters under the twinkle lights the Montgomerys have strung up around the vicinity.

"My name is Bizzy. We met the night of—Ginger King's

lecture on how to land a man." I wince because she knows all too well what else happened that night. "I work at the inn. I'm Nessa's friend." That last part comes out softer with the under-pinnings of defeat. I'm not sure Nessa will score me any points with her.

Chelsea gasps. Her mouth rounds out in a hard O and the strawberry-colored gloss on her lips shimmers as well.

I should run. She forces a tight smile to stretch across her face, the kind you give to people you don't really want to see.

"Right." She cradles her phone to her chest. "I do remember you. That was a terrible night." Her expression dissolves to palpable grief, and this time it looks genuine. "I lost my best friend." She sniffs into the back of her hand. "I'm sorry. I'm a mess. I'm sure you're wondering what I'm doing here." She hikes her phone into the air as if she were about to pitch it. "Shel is gone, but the show must go on. I know she'd want me to keep posting. It's what we do. It was in her blood." She takes a deep breath. "I was just getting a bunch of shots to put out slowly over the month. I'm not posting again until after the funeral next week. Her mother has already made the arrangements. Any word on who could have done this? I mean, I heard what happened at the inn last month. You don't think there's a serial killer running loose in Cider Cove, do you?" Sherlock yelps and moans. "Hey." She looks down and gives him a quick pat. "It's okay, handsome. I think you're safe."

"I'm hoping we're all safe," I say. "And no—the two killings aren't related. There was an arrest made in the last homicide case. The killer was apprehended. Just like this one will be, too."

The whites of her eyes flash my way.

I'm not exactly rooting for that.

I tip my head her way, examining her features. Why in the world would she say that if she wasn't the killer? I have to find Jasper. I have to let him know she's all but implicated herself. Of course, I can't do that without implicating *myself* in the process.

Nope, I can't do that. But I will most certainly point a finger in her direction.

"Chelsea, you were closest to Shelby. Do you know if she had any enemies? I mean, did you think she was easy to get along with?"

A sharp bout of laughter bounces from her. "I guess you didn't know Shelby. Yes, she could be sweet when she wanted to be— but let's just say she had a very sharp edge to her. Personally, I knew what to expect, so most of the time I was prepared to look the other way." *Except when I couldn't because a prison sentence loomed in the balance.* Her expression sours. "Shelby came from money. I didn't. Life was a bit of a joke to her in that respect. I had to work hard for everything I have." She sighs. "That's why I felt so bad when she wanted to mess with Scout. She was our friend. She was just trying to pay her rent, and Shelby thought we should take her down a notch before she got too big for her britches."

I wrinkle my nose. "Nessa mentioned something about that. I guess you were rivals?" I ask, trying to recall the conversation.

Chelsea rolls her eyes as the twinkle lights reflect off her face. "Hardly. She was just getting started, amassing followers, taking the best pictures she knew how. She just started to dabble in video. Anyway—Scout said she would have a meet and greet for anyone who was up for it at the pier. She said she'd bring each person who came a Mason jar filled with love and light." She averts her eyes. "That's sort of her thing—blue Mason jars filled with tiny lights and paper butterflies. Only about thirty or so people said they could make it, and she wasn't expecting a huge crowd to begin with. Shelby thought it would be hilarious to have our own followers RSVP."

"Oh no," I say, pressing my hand to my chest in anticipation of how this might have played out. Even Sherlock cowers as if he had a hunch it wasn't good.

Chelsea nods. "*Oh no* is right. We got close to two thousand local fans to RSVP. Poor Scout went ahead with it. She ordered thousands of Mason jars. She filled them with those pricey battery-operated lights and cut out all the butterflies herself from glittery paper that I'm told cost a fortune. Anyway, per Shelby's orders, our fans didn't show up after all. Scout not only took a big financial hit purchasing all the supplies for the event, but she was humiliated all over the Internet. She was a laughing stock. There are pictures of her with crates of Mason jars just sitting alone on the waterfront. Her career as an influencer was over before it really began. But, Shelby being Shelby told Scout to grow up and get over it. She's the one that suggested Scout go into PR. And then she hand-fed her Ginger King. Ginger and Shelby go way back. And apparently, Shelby has some magical pull with her because Ginger agreed to hire Scout even though she didn't have a drop of experience in the PR arena."

"That's an interesting turn of events. It almost sounds as if Shelby wanted Scout to succeed at something after all—just not the very thing she was doing herself."

She shakes out her bun and her blonde locks fall to her shoulders. "You nailed it. But believe me, Scout wanted revenge. Shelby might have thrown out a peace offering by way of Ginger, but Scout's blood was still boiling."

"You don't think Scout was capable of hurting Shelby like that, do you?"

"I don't know." Her gaze flits to the woods just beyond the festivities. "She was angry, yes. But she seemed to have moved on. I think Ginger was probably closer to pegging the killer when she accused Nessa. I'm sorry, I know you work together, but that girl is a real mess. She started sending Shelby these hate-filled texts and harassed her every chance she got. It was getting really bad these last few weeks. I guess her family is in a lot of trouble with that loan they took out." She shrugs as if offering a third party apology.

"How would that be Shelby's fault?" I shake my head, trying to wrap my mind around it.

"It wasn't." Chelsea smacks her lips. "Okay, so maybe it was a little. Shelby never really thought that much of Nessa. I did hear her say something about telling her dad he could make a lot of money off those idiots." She says *idiots* in air quotes.

My stomach sinks when she says it. I've known Nessa and her sister, Vera, for as long as I can remember. Vera might be a proverbial mean girl, but Nessa and I have always gotten along. And their parents are good, honest people. It burns me to think Shelby would call them idiots.

"Look"—Chelsea pulls her cider close and takes a sip—"I'm sorry to have said any of that. I'm still reeling from the fact my best friend is dead."

Sherlock runs his forehead over my knee. *Nessa said Shelby did something to this girl, too. Get the story out of her, Bizzy.*

I nod quickly his way. "Chelsea, it sounds as if Shelby had a bit of a dark side. Did she ever do anything to you personally?"

Her expression hardens to flint as her eyes grow cold.

A heavy sigh expels from her. "She did. And you know what? She made me promise to never tell." A dull laugh presses from her. "A part of me wants to give her that. Besides, if I tell the truth now, people will simply think I'm trying to save face and ruining Shel's reputation at the very same time." She shudders. "I guess the window has closed on that opportunity and I'll have to live with it."

Sherlock groans, *That sounded morbid. Whatever it was, it was something big, Bizzy. Big, I tell you.*

I give a slight nod. "It sounds as if you're not ready to go there. I hope you can find some peace with whatever it was."

Her eyes glint with tears for the very first time, and I do believe they are all for her. I haven't seen her shed a single tear for Shelby yet.

"I hope so, too," she whispers.

I try my hardest to tune into her thoughts, but there's nothing but arid space—something akin to a vegetative state. Whatever has her riled up, it's almost as if it has the power to put her into a trance.

"Chelsea, who do you think did this?" *Did you do it?* I ask the silent question as her eyes meet with mine.

"I don't know. If it wasn't Nessa, maybe—maybe it was Carter." She shrugs as if it were wholly probable.

"Carter?"

"Carter O'Riley." She nods. "He runs that matchmaking service for men."

"Oh, that's right. The dark-haired man. Her ex. He was there that night. In fact, he said something to upset her." I try my hardest to reflect on him. Wait a minute. He was begging for her to give him a moment of her time—internally at least. A thought comes to me. "Shelby said something to the effect that he could thank her for the best career move he's made. I think she said something about him cheating on her." I bring my fingers to my mouth as I realize that she said that last tidbit to herself.

"He did cheat on her—with *Ginger*. Which was terrible because the four of us were close for a long time. We did everything together, racket ball, sailing, safety courses at the shooting range, cooking classes, yoga."

"Four of you?"

"Shelby, Ginger, Nessa, and me." She shrugs into the crowd. "Anyway, Shel and Carter were a train wreck from the beginning. And then she found Luke." She makes a face. ***Not that he was any better.***

"Carter O'Riley," I say again, trying my best to remember every detail I might already know about him. "Why would you think Carter had anything to do with this?"

"*Please*. He was obsessed with Shelby. Everyone knows that. And Shelby still very much had a thing for him. I think if her anger ever had the chance to subside, she'd have gotten back together with him."

"But she had a new boyfriend."

Chelsea shakes her head. "Luke blew it. She was ten times as angry with him as she ever was Carter. And whatever set her off, she just found out about it, too. She said she would give me all the gory details later that night—but later that night—Shelby came to an end."

An owl hoots in the distance and a chill runs down to my bones.

"I'd better get going." She offers a forlorn smile. "Tell Nessa I said hello."

Heaven knows I won't be seeing Nessa again anytime soon. I think I'll steer clear of a lot of people until the smoke clears. Not that it ever clears with Shelby. Nope. I'll be living with this nightmare for the rest of my life.

She takes off and I'm left in her wake trying to make sense of the jagged pieces she just laid at my feet.

Shelby's ex-boyfriend, Carter, was obsessed with her. He wanted her back. Her current boyfriend, Luke, had done something very bad—and Shelby had just found out about it that night. Scout—well, she was humiliated. And Chelsea? She was sworn to secrecy. She said if she told the truth, people would think she were trying to save face and that she would be ruining Shelby's reputation at the very same time. And, of course, there's Nessa. Poor Nessa. I wish she never knew them.

I shake my head at it all just as Sherlock jerks the leash in my hand.

He's here, Bizzy! He's here! I can smell him. He smells like pine trees and toothpaste!

"Who's here?" A laugh bubbles from me. I struggle to keep up as Sherlock navigates us through the crowd and straight over toward the haunted hayrides.

No sooner do we get to the front of the line than I see a

certain drop-dead gorgeous homicide detective helping someone down from the tractor trailer stacked with bales of hay.

Forever a prince.

A giggle gets trapped in my throat as I speed his way.

I give a wild wave as I try to garner his attention and Sherlock barks and jumps as if doing the same.

Jasper looks this way, his gray eyes flashing in the night like stars before he does a double take. Only he's not smiling like a loon the way I am.

And then the bigger picture comes in clear as the woman he's helping down looks my way as well.

Sherlock leads me right into their midst and my feet follow along like a couple of traitors.

"Well, if it isn't Bizzy Barker." Camila offers a bemused smile.

It's the kind of smile that says *I've bested you. I've won. You are the butt of the joke and we've already laughed because of it.*

It's the kind of smile that makes my stomach sour, makes me want to turn and run away. The exact kind of smile that both boils my blood and makes me want to cry.

Jasper steps over in haste, and Sherlock goes wild until he's happily jumping on his owner. But Jasper hardly offers him a quick pat.

"Bizzy, it's not what it looks like."

I blink back with surprise. "It's exactly what it looks like." I force myself to manufacture a tight smile, but it comes out more of a grimace. "You were having a good time with a friend." It took everything in me to push those words out. "I'll see you both at the inn." I take off so fast, poor Sherlock has to run to keep up with me.

I find Emmie and spill everything in spastic half-sentences on the way to the car.

Emmie doesn't say *I told you so.*

She thinks it.

CHAPTER 7

J couldn't sleep all night.

Jasper came straight to my door once he got back to the inn, but I kept the lights off and stayed under the covers pretending to be fast asleep. Of course, he called and texted, but I shut my phone off as soon as I saw him and Camila together getting off of the haunted hayride. If it wasn't apparent before that Camila wants to hit the hay with him, it is now.

As much as I want to be incensed, livid, *fit to kill*—I'm mostly emotionally wounded from the entire experience. I've never been big on either humiliation or rejection, and whether or not he meant to do it, Jasper Wilder doled out a huge helping of both.

The Cottage Café is bustling with tourists and townspeople alike this morning. And each and every one of them is clamoring to order the pumpkin spice mini muffins by the dozens. Not that I could blame them. Emmie and I worked hard to get that special spark in the recipe. She mixed and baked, and I stayed at the far end of the kitchen encouraging her lest I cast an inadvertent pox on the batch at hand. I would give anything if I could bake like Emmie. Baking was my singular obsession for as long as I could remember, and yet I've only managed to char or undercook anything I dared to put into an oven. And sometimes when I'm really good, I can do both.

My sweet cat, Fish, sits at the base of the counter as if standing guard over the seaside café. Sherlock Bones stayed out by the front desk with Peanut and Nessa. Those cute pooches put a smile on everyone's face that sees them. And I'd swear on my life that they're drumming up more business as well.

Georgie alert. Fish runs right over to the walking, talking human kaftan and Georgie is quick to scoop her up into her arms.

"What can I get for you, Georgie?" A weak smile floats to my lips, something I probably couldn't have achieved for anyone other than my sweet yet zany friend.

Georgie's hair is frazzled, her lips are painted a deep shade of pumpkin, and with that long purple and black dress on, she looks as if she's getting into the spirit of the haunted season.

"Have you ever seen so many people?" she practically mouths the words as she gawks at the crowded café.

"Never," I say, reaching over to pet Fish. "And I think it has every bit as much to do with the animals than it has to do with those pumpkin spice magic muffins we're selling out of."

Fish arches her back and purrs at the thought. *I am a show-stopper, Bizzy. The dogs aren't so bad themselves.*

Georgie shakes her head as if she heard the tiny cat. "It's not the pets—and it's not any dark magic you might be brewing in the kitchen." She leans in, her eyes expanding wide. "It's the *murder.*"

"What?" I squawk without meaning to as I give a nervous glance to the crowd. As the manager of the Country Cottage Inn, it's my job to make sure this place is looked at in a positive light, and murder isn't anywhere near the list of things I'd like for this establishment to be known for.

I glance to the stormy looking ocean just beyond the beach out front. Most people who stay at the inn love to buy a cup of hot cider and walk the sandy bay just outside the café. They come for the cozy cottages, the cobbled old-world feel that the grounds offer, the ivy covered walls, the people, the pets—but murder? "I'm sorry. I just can't wrap my head around it."

"You don't have to." Georgie waves me off. "I've heard whispers all up and down Main Street. Now that I'm working on that mural for the city, I'm in the know with all the good and *deadly* gossip." Her eyes narrow in on mine. "Speaking of which, a little birdie named Emmie told me you found a certain detective cavorting with a certain ex-girlfriend. I say we shank her, Bizzy. I'll get her in a dark corner and you come at her with a broken bottle!"

"No, thank you. Trust me, Georgie. She's not worth prison." I shoot a look to the corner of the café where Camila sits diligently clacking away at her laptop. I have no idea what she's doing or why she isn't at the high school out in Sheffield where she's supposedly a counselor. I'm beginning to think everything about her is a fraud and the only genuine thing is the fact she wants to steal Jasper. Although, I guess she didn't have to steal. I'm guessing he went on that haunted hayride willingly. Who knew the only one that would be frightened last night would be me? And I wasn't even on the darn ride.

"It's true. Jasper and I are over," I say it lower than a whisper, but Camila lifts a brow in this direction anyway.

Figures. She's had her antennae up the entire time. I bet she called in sick today just to hear me say those words. She's working overtime, all right—to ruin my life.

I haven't dared to pry into her thoughts. The only time I'm bombarded with unwanted mental musings is when I'm about to pop with stress. And believe you me, with another homicide, an ex-girlfriend, and a mind reading deputy underfoot, I'm just about there.

"*What*? You and Jasper, over? Just like that?" Georgie looks enraged by the thought. "You can't just give up. You fight for your man, Bizzy Baker. That woman doesn't have a ring on her finger. And you don't stop until you get one."

I catch a quick glimpse of Camila rolling her eyes and I'm tempted to do the same.

"Besides"—Georgie all but pushes Fish into her chest—"tonight's the art show out in Seaview. I'm going and so is Macy, and both your mother and your father. Do you want to be the only Baker left out of the equation?"

I make a face. "You forgot my brother. Hux isn't going either."

"Okay, do you want to be the only *important* family member of your family who isn't present?"

A laugh percolates right out of me just as a dark-haired deputy strolls on in.

"Not this again," I mutter as he steps up to the counter. "Leo." I nod over to him. "You remember Georgie."

Georgie waves me off. "Leo and I have become fast friends. He caught me behind my cottage hammering away at a bag of glass bottles and tried to wrestle me to the ground."

Leo grimaces. He's comely, some might say handsome, but I'm not getting suckered into that again. Besides, my compass is still firmly set in a Wilder direction—perhaps unwisely so.

Leo nods to her. "And I want to apologize again, Georgie. By the way, I drove past Main Street and I can see the vision you have for the mural. I can't wait to see the finished product."

"Oh, you will, you sly handsome dude. You will." She gives a flirtatious wink. "Anytime you're up for another wrestling match, let me know, big boy." She looks my way. "You'll be at the art show tonight, Bizzy, because I said so. It's at seven. We can't be late. And yes, Detective Baker, that means you're my ride. You know my night vision is atrocious. I can't tell the difference between a skunk and oncoming traffic and, believe me, I've run across that test one too many times. I'll see you later."

I come around the counter and take Fish from her as she takes off.

"Follow me," I say to Leo as we find a seat near the window.

His lips curl and his dark eyes widen a notch as if he were finally getting what he wanted.

"You said we were transmundane." I tip my head to the side.

Fish squirms as she struggles to get a better look at him. *How can you trust those eyes, Bizzy? It's clear he's trying to bewitch you.*

Deputy Granger belts out a laugh before reaching over and touching her ear.

"I'm not bewitching anyone." He nods to me. "And we're not witches." He sighs over at Fish. "I'm just like Bizzy. I can hear you. And I think you're sweet and special. Not all cats are as friendly as you are."

Fish purrs on cue. *Ooh, I like him, Bizzy. Give him an extra piece of bacon, too.*

I make a face as I look to Leo. "That's her way of likening you to a dog. Now extrapolate on that transmundane thing, would you?"

Camila turns around and does a double take in our direction.

Leo follows my gaze and gives a long blink.

"Don't worry about her," he says. "And if you're wondering— the reason I ended it with her was because she thought of Jasper more than she did me." He leans forward and folds his hands together. "I guess that's when this gift turns into a curse. It has a way of interfering with every relationship I've ever had."

"Well, if the rumors are true, you took her on even though she was with your best friend. That's no man's land as far as unwritten rules go."

He gives a wry smile. "I've always learned my lessons the hard way. I'm not saying it's my best feature. It turns out, I threw away a lifelong friendship for nothing."

"I'm sorry to hear that. Maybe you and Jasper can work things out in the future?"

He shrugs "Onto bigger issues at hand. Does anyone in your family have the same ability as you?"

"No. Mayor Woods and I were friends in middle school right up until she pushed me into a whiskey barrel and tried to drown me. Three things happened that day—I became fiercely afraid of both water and confined spaces, I removed Mack Woods from my friend list, and I have been prying into other people's minds without meaning to ever since."

"An accident." He nods. "It's happened before according to my aunt. But be warned, should you have children they might inherit your ability regardless of the fact. They think it's some sort of sixth sense inside all of us, but for whatever reason, it flourishes in very few. And you, Bizzy Baker, are among the elite."

"The transmundane elite." I nod as I try to take this in. "So, this is some kind of a superpower?"

Fish taps her paw to my chest. *I knew you were special, Bizzy. We need to have Georgie fashion a cape for you out of one of her dresses. The pink one with all the gold sparkles! You'll be Captain Bizzy, and I'll be your perceptive, yet adorable sidekick.*

A small giggle bounces through me. "You are both perceptive and adorable. No cape for me," I say, landing a quick kiss to Fish's little pink nose.

Leo tips his head. "I don't know. Fish might be onto something. I think both you and I can use our powers for good. But before we go there, I want you to know a little bit more of what these powers mean. Yes, we're transmundane, but we're further classified as telesensuals, or telepaths. Plainly stated, people who can read the thoughts of others."

"Telesensual," I say, letting the foreign word roll off my tongue for the very first time. "I like it. Maybe more than telepath. So if we're a classification, that must mean there are other classifications. What are they? Do you know?"

"I do." He leans in just as a hand falls over his shoulder.

"Mind if I cut in?" a deep voice strums and we both look up to find Jasper looking like a deity with diamond eyes, and I can't help but smile—albeit short-lived.

Leo makes a face at me because obviously he doesn't agree with my description.

Fish chortles to herself. *He looks good and jealous, Bizzy. I think you have him where you want him. Good move. Leo, why don't we check on those ornery dogs and make sure they haven't chewed the furniture to matchsticks? It might be a dog's life, but around here a cat's duty is never done.*

She bounces out of my arms and onto the floor and Leo nods to both Jasper and me as he follows Fish right back into the main hall of the inn.

"Bizzy." Jasper falls into the seat, his eyes glued to mine. He's so stunningly handsome my stomach squeezes tightly at the sight of him. Never mind the fact my lips are suddenly having a serious craving for one of his lingering kisses. "I promise you. It's not what it looked like." His brows are furrowed and he looks ten times more vexingly handsome now that he's distressed than he ever has before. So not fair.

I glance over and catch a glimpse of Camila frowning in this direction.

"You'd better hurry with your excuses. Your girlfriend looks as if she's getting miffed."

His cheek lifts, no smile. "Would you believe my mother was involved in that mess yesterday?"

My mouth opens for a moment. "Why, yes, I would." It's no secret Gwyneth is rooting for Camila to win over Jasper's heart.

"Good. Because she asked me to meet her at the fair when I got off work. It seemed innocent enough. She invited me to dinner. We had bratwurst." His brows lift as if the bratwurst were just as much to blame as his mother. "Camila showed up out of the blue, said a quick hello, and took off to stand in line for the hayride. A few minutes later, my mother discovered Camila left her phone on the table—yet suddenly had an emergency."

I nod, seeing clearly how he got from point A to thorny-horny point C, as in Camila. "And you were kind enough to take it to her."

He winces. "Once I got there, she confessed to accidently buying two tickets and she was next up in line."

"And you hopped right onto the Haunted Ex-Girlfriend Express." I shrink in my seat. "Sorry, I couldn't help it."

"I refused to go." He shakes his head. "But she suggested it could be a good opportunity to talk so we could both move on without any strain between us."

I bite down over my lip as I cast another quick glance her way. "That sounds reasonable—I guess."

"It wasn't." Jasper takes a deep breath. "With all the other people screaming their heads off, we couldn't get a word in edgewise."

"Let me guess. She was so afraid herself, she hopped right onto your lap."

His eyes widen a notch. *It's like she was there. And how I wish I wasn't.*

He gives a reluctant nod. "It's true. But believe me, Bizzy, that's when things came into focus and I put the manipulated pieces together." *And if I lose Bizzy over this, I will never forgive myself for being so gullible.*

A breath escapes me as I fill with relief, but my head and my heart are in two different places.

"Look, Jasper, you and Camila had something for a very long time. I'm just someone you met a month ago." My heart sinks as I relegate myself to such a trivial shelf. "I think maybe the two of you should talk so that you're not in a strained place. I mean, we're not officially together or anything." Again, my heart aches as if it were about to explode. Of course, I want to be official with Jasper, but I have a feeling Camila will pull out all the stops to make sure that won't happen.

"We can be." He reaches over and picks up my hand. "Bizzy, I don't care if I've known you a month or ten years. I feel very strongly about you. And I don't want to walk away from what we have."

"Then don't. But do talk to Camila. Whenever you're ready to do so, and might I suggest, you choose the venue." I take a moment to frown over at her. "I just need your heart and your mind to be clear and open to another relationship and hopefully one with me. But if you decide to give it another go with Camila, I will totally understand that as well."

Liar, liar, Bizzy Baker on fire.

I press out a short-lived smile.

Jasper shakes his head, those lightning bolt eyes of his still very much pinned to mine. "I'll talk to Camila, but only to bring closure to an already closed-off situation. I'm not remotely inter-ested in her that way anymore." His thumb bounces over my hand. "Tonight's my sister's big showing down in Seaview. I hope you haven't changed your mind about coming. You'll be my date. We'll drive out together."

I bite down on my lip to keep from grinning like a loon who was just asked to the dance by the cute boy in class—even though it's true in every adolescent sense.

"Okay. But would you mind if another person tagged along with us?"

He tips his head to the side. *As long as it's not Leo Granger.*

"It's Georgie," I mouth her name and his chest bounces with relief.

"I guess it's a double date then. I'll pick you up at six-thirty?"

"Sounds good."

He sits back a moment. *A part of me wants to discuss the case with her, but another very real part of me doesn't want to drag Bizzy into danger. I know she's interested. But I'm too interested in keeping her safe to go there. Besides, once she sees who else will be at the showing tonight, I'm pretty sure her natural thirst for justice will take over.*

"I'll swing by the cottage at six-thirty. I've got to run to the office." Jasper pulls me up and lands a chaste kiss to my lips before taking off and leaving both my lips and curiosity thirsty for more.

Who could be showing up tonight that has the ability to foster my thirst for justice?

I suck in a quick breath as it hits me.

A suspect!

Perfect. I'll have a romantic date with Jasper tonight *and* a shot at discovering who killed Shelby Harris.

A breeze filled with sugary perfume takes over my senses just as Camila strides up.

"I guess I'll see you at the showing tonight, Bizzy." Her lips curve with a malevolent smile. "Jasper's sister, Ella, and I are such good friends." ***And by the time I'm through with Jasper, he won't know what hit him. Neither will you, Dizzy Baker.***

Her fingers flicker my way as she waves goodbye.

A date, a suspect, and an obnoxious ex-girlfriend.

I'm looking forward to two out of three.

That's not bad.

But something tells me Camila Ryder is bad to the bone indeed.

CHAPTER 8

*T*he Seaview County Museum of Art is a stunning building with a water display out front that shoots two stories into the sky. Inside, it's polished and cosmopolitan, with expansive ceilings and a cavernous maze layout laden with over-sized acrylic and oil paintings, all of which I'm looking forward to spending time admiring.

Georgie hits the ground running as soon as we step inside the brightly lit museum, but Jasper pulls me to the side, that naughty smile twitching on his lips as he presses his gaze to mine.

"Have I told you how stunning you look tonight?" The scent of his thick, spiced cologne has the power to hypnotize me just about as much as his eyes.

"Only sixteen times on the way over. Georgie is beginning to wonder if I've fractured your mind."

A dull moan evicts from him. "Would you think less of me if I said you've fractured my mind and body?"

A laugh bounces from me. "I'm not sure how to take that. But if I can kiss it and make it feel better, let me know."

"I'm officially putting you on notice."

"What's this?" a female voice calls from behind and we turn to

DOG DAYS OF MURDER

find the artist herself looking adorable in an A-line denim dress that accentuates her baby bump. She laughs as she pulls Jasper into a brief embrace. "Bizzy, I knew my brother was smitten, but I've never seen him like this." She leans in. "Don't tell Camila I said so." She winces as she looks to Jasper. "Does she know about Camila?"

"I do," I say. "In fact, she's staying—"

"Right here." Camila herself pops into our midst. "Jasper, that picture Ella did of us is on display in the ballroom." She bites down on a devious crimson smile as her gaze slants my way a moment. "You must come and see it with me." She takes him by the hand and Ella is quick to navigate them in that direction.

"Bizzy?" he calls out for me.

"I'll be right there," I say.

Maybe. Most likely not.

I make a face at the polished looking crowd. Everyone looks as if they were shipped in from upper Manhattan—and here I'm wearing my jeans and my favorite ruby red pea coat. Granted. I've donned my thigh-high black suede boots, which are borderline edgy and one hundred percent sexy, but a part of me still thinks I should have vetted my wardrobe choices a bit more.

A familiar face waves to me from deeper into the room, and I'm more than relieved to see Macy standing there with a fruity looking cocktail in hand so I speed over to her.

"See anything you like?" I ask as we take in the crowd. The paintings themselves are all tucked away in offshoot to the main hall, so I haven't had the chance to ogle one just yet.

Macy gurgles with a dark laugh. "I see everything I like. Who knew Jasper's sister specialized in kink?"

"In what?" My entire body grows rigid as I struggle to cast my eyes on a single oversized canvas.

"*Nudes*." Macy practically hisses the words, "As in naked dudes and chicks."

85

"No kidding?" A horrible thought hits me. "Oh my goodness. I'm going to faint or vomit."

Macy clicks her tongue at me. "Who knew my baby sis would grow up to be such a prude?"

"Trust me, Macy. I'm no prude. Jasper's ex just dragged him off to look at a painting that Ella did of the two of them."

"*Eww.*" Macy looks as if she could puke, too, if she wanted. "Never mind that"—she shudders—"let's focus on something far more important. *Me.*" She blinks a hot pink smile. "Guess what?"

"I'm afraid to ask." As of late, there have been an awful lot of surprises. But it will take a lot to top a nude picture of Jasper and Camila.

"That group of hunky hotties who were at Ginger's seminar the other night? They're here in number. And they are all single and ready to mingle."

"What hunky hotties?" I suck in a quick breath as it comes to me. "Carter O'Riley and his testosterone squad?"

"Yup." Macy rocks back on her heels, licking her lips as if she were about to take a bite out of some serious beefcake. "And you can bet your mini muffins I'm taking one home with me."

I'm quick to swat her. "No, you're not. You don't even know their names. Don't take anybody home. Or I might be moved to kill you."

Macy glowers at something just beyond me. "Rumor has it, our mother has been taking home a certain someone."

I suck in another sharp breath. At this rate, I'm liable to inhale every canvas in this place before the night is through. Although, if that's what it takes to keep me from seeing Jasper and Camila's nude review, then I might be all for it.

I turn to find Mom laughing and having a wonderful time with Max Wilder strapped to her side.

"They look so cute together," I muse. Mom looks elegant in a simple black dress and Max has donned a dark suit—looking eerily like Jasper's twin in the process. "My goodness, that's not Jasper, is it?" I'm only half-kidding. It's a mind-bender of another dimension when your own mother is getting hot and heavy with a look-alike of the man you're hoping to get hot and heavy with yourself. I'm sure there's a special place in a psychiatrist's office for people like me.

"Let's find out if it's your man." Macy threads her arm through mine and speeds us over.

Mom's eyes widen a moment. "Hello, girls. Isn't this wonderful?" She lifts the champagne flute a notch and her arm flails as if she were slightly tipsy—and I'm betting she is. My mother is notoriously bad at holding her liquor.

We exchange polite hellos and Max—who looks suspiciously a heck of a lot more like Jasper tonight than he did the other day —leans in.

"Have the two of you met the rest of the family?"

"I've met your mother," I volunteer, and for reasons that escape me, it comes out with a little laugh.

Macy nods. "And we've met your sister."

Max lifts a brow to Macy. "Your mother says you're anxious to meet my brothers."

A low, level growl emits from her. "Say goodbye to my mother, Max. Tonight, she dies a slow and painful death."

His brows twitch the exact way Jasper's are prone to do. "If you promise to spare her life, I'll introduce you to the two of them tonight."

Macy perks to life. "Mommy, have I mentioned how much I love your new boyfriend? He's so charming and sweet, and I bet he has exquisite taste in siblings."

We share a warm laugh at my sister's lunacy.

No sooner does Max propose the scenario than he plucks two more Jasper look-alikes from the crowd.

"Bizzy, Macy—this is my brother, Dalton." He points to the one whose hair has a touch more auburn to it, but the same warm smile, same stunning gray eyes. "Dalton is the head football coach at Ward University."

Macy's lips twitch with delight as she extends a hand his way. "What a coincidence. Both my sister and I went to Ward. Home run," she says, indulging in a hearty shake.

I lean in and whisper, "I think you mean touchdown."

Macy wrinkles her nose. "Oh, he'll get that out of me, too."

Dalton belts out a laugh. *That's what I'm counting on, sweetheart.*

Mom and I exchange a look but for entirely different reasons.

"And this"—Max pulls the darker-haired Jasper look-alike forward, only his eyes are blue through and through—"is Jamison. Attorney at law. Need to sue? See this guy right here." He leans in. "Need to win? Maybe see your brother."

And I'm only partly teasing. Max slaps his brother on the back.

A small laugh titters in our circle.

Jamison offers us both a friendly shake. "Nice to meet you both." He gives a wistful shake of the head my way. "Bizzy, you've stolen my brother's sanity. Maybe the Wilders should look into suing *you.*"

Another round of riotous laughter breaks out.

Jamison's eyes linger over me for a moment. *Jasper always was the smart one. If he loses this one, I might have to sue him for stupidity.*

I offer a polite nod his way. I think I just found my favorite brother.

And soon enough, my sister pulls both Dalton and Jamison to the side. If I'm not mistaken, it looks as if she's conducting some sort of thorough interview with the two of them.

Figures.

My sister has always been one to cut right to the chase. Macy wants to snag herself a Wilder brother, and there are very few things in life that my sister goes after and doesn't come away the victor.

Mom and Max lean in, getting all moony-eyed and whispering things that illicit a very dirty grin in each of them, and my feet can't carry me away fast enough.

Good grief.

If I had known Jasper was going to ditch me for his ex, I would have stayed home.

A pair of arms wraps themselves around my waist, and I turn to find Jasper Wilder offering up a sheepish grin.

"I see you met my brothers. I'm sorry. I was on my way over and my mother waylaid me."

Why do I get the feeling Camila and Gwyneth are working in tandem to keep us apart?

Jasper winces. *I shouldn't have said that. She's going to think my mother is rooting for Camila.* He frowns just past me. *She might be, but I'll be the last to tell Bizzy.*

My mouth falls open. But before I can wrap my brain around his brutal honesty, I spot an all too familiar ex-boyfriend who happened to belong to Shelby Harris at one time.

"Jasper, look," I whisper. "Carter is here. He's the suspect you were hinting at, isn't he?"

A dark laugh brews in his chest as he turns to see him. "That's what I like about you, Bizzy. There is no mystery too small that you won't solve. Yes, that's the suspect du jour for the evening. But I don't want either of us to press him."

"What? Jasper, this is the perfect opportunity to do so. He's all but ours for the taking."

He frowns in that direction. "Have you seen my sister's work yet?"

"Her work?" I glance around suspiciously. "No, but I'm sure every piece is lovely. Let's go." I try to wrangle him in that direction, but he pivots us into an enclave instead.

"Wow." I press my face to his shoulder a moment. "Jasper, they're all naked."

"That they are."

I slowly pry my lids open. "And they're so—very lifelike."

"And that they are, too."

"Jasper, you said she painted you and Camila." A horrible groan comes from me without meaning to. "I refuse to see that. Please tell me you didn't pose for a sitting."

"No." A set of comma-like dimples appears on either side of his mouth. "And—well, I think the painting should speak for itself."

He navigates us over to the next installment space.

"I can't look," I wail, trying my best to walk with my eyes closed.

"I promise you will not have a problem with it."

"That's what you think. And by the way, I'm beginning to wonder about *how* you think."

He pulls me close and his chest bounces against my side. "Open."

My lids flutter slowly and, sure enough, we're standing in front of an oversized canvas that takes up nearly the entire wall. It's a dark landscape—a little hard to make out. It looks like head-stones and a hillside along with a charred tree of some sort.

"Jasper, is this a scene from a cemetery?"

He nods as he stares out at it.

I squint at it. "And are those a couple of bats in the tree?"

"That would be correct."

I take in the picture in its totality, and it looks straight from the scene of some Halloween nightmare with ghosts and pump-kins and even a hand coming up out of a grave.

"Wait a minute," I say. "You're the bats?"

"We're the bats." He leans in. "If you look closely, you'll see Camila has horns and a tail."

My fingers float to my lips to keep from laughing. "Oh, Jasper. Why do I get the feeling Ella isn't Camila's biggest fan?"

"Because you're intuitive." He pulls me in tight and a naughty grin slides up one side of his face once again. "I'm sure Camila wanted you to think the worst. And perhaps her intentions are to land us back together. But I promise, there is nothing anyone can do to take me away from you."

The sound of heels clacking this way erupts just as his mother appears at the entry to the alcove.

"Jasper?" Gwyneth's dark hair is pulled back, she's clad in black, save for the caustic shade of red lipstick, and she happens to sneer when she sees us locked in an embrace. "Hello, Bizzy." Her expression falls flat. "Jasper, your sister needs help unloading a few items from her car. She brought trinkets for the guests. Apparently, there are several of them. Your brothers suggested I find you."

Jasper's chest expands. "I'll be right back."

"And I'll"—I point back to the haunted painting—"be hanging out with the lovebirds."

He offers a quick peck to my cheek before taking off with his mother.

And that's my cue. I tiptoe to the front of the alcove, happy to see he's already out of sight. I spot Carter right away in the crowd over by the refreshment table where an entire throng of men is capitalizing off both the moment and their hormones as they speak to a gaggle of girls. He's dressed in a suit, although he looks as if he's uncomfortable in his own skin at the moment and I wonder if it's because he's grieving.

Figures. Carter probably has his men stalking all sorts of intellectual events where hot, young women are prone to congregate. He's a predator. But at the moment he's all by his lonesome, so I step on over before the window closes on my Jasper-free moment.

"Carter," I say breathless as I step in his path before he launches in another direction. "I think we met at that"—I wince—"Ginger's talk on how to catch a man."

"Oh." Any trace of a smile quickly evaporates from his face. "At the mixer."

"Yes. I'm actually the manager of the Country Cottage Inn, so I make it a point to recognize guests. You were there with your men that night." I give a little shrug.

Carter closes his eyes a moment as if reliving it. "That was a nightmare. I'm sorry. Not the mixer—but, well—you know."

"Yes, I do know." I step in. "Were you close to Shelby?" I'm not letting him see all of my cards. I'll leave it to him to tell me.

"*Close*? We were engaged at one point. She was my everything." His jaw clenches. "She still is."

Still is?

He obviously has very strong feelings for her.

"I'm sorry. Can I ask what went wrong?" I shrug a little. "I mean, sometimes it helps to talk about it. And you look pretty upset."

"I am upset, and I don't mind. In fact, Shelby has always been my world. The reason we spilt had to do with commitment. I kept pushing back the wedding date and she called my bluff. And by the time she walked out of my life, I couldn't have wanted her more. I would have done anything to keep her in it, and now it's too late."

"I'm sorry. That must be terribly painful." I study him a moment. "What did you think of this new guy she was seeing?"

"*Luke?*" he says his name like it was a four-letter word of another color. "The guy is a joke. He's some auto mechanic she met when her car was in the shop, and the next thing you know he's wearing a suit, running the new loan department of Harris Financial."

"Really?" I blink back. "He must have been qualified. I mean, they wouldn't just put someone in charge like that without any background in finance, would they?"

"You have no idea the pull Shelby had with her father. She could have plugged anyone she wanted into any part of that firm. And she did. And do you know why she did it? Revenge. She went out and found the first guy she could once she broke things off with me because she knew it would infuriate me. She was right." He shoves his hands into his pockets. His demeanor shifts from pained to full of a percolating rage. "I'm sorry she's gone." *But at least now he can't have her. He never deserved her in the first place.*

I press my hand to my chest as I take a step back. Chelsea mentioned he was obsessed. Maybe Carter killed her because she was with Luke?

"Carter, do you know Nessa Crosby? She works at the inn."

"Nessa?" He looks momentarily startled. "Yes, of course, I know Nessa. I was with Shelby before things went south between the two of them." His chest expands and he inspects me. "We used to be good friends."

I wonder if she's got news on Nessa's arrest? It should have happened by now. Of course, with the bumbling Seaview Sheriff's Department botching the investigation it could take a decade.

He postures toward me. "Why do you ask about Nessa?"

"Just wondering." My shoulders hike a notch. "She knew Shelby as well. She's pretty upset."

My goodness, does Carter think Nessa did it?

My eyes widen with my next thought. Or did Carter steal the gun and kill Shelby, hoping to frame Nessa with the crime?

Carter nods as if he were putting the pieces together. "I'll stop by some time and see how she's doing. I really do care about Nessa." *And that's exactly why I'll be working hard on her defense. As soon as they slap those cuffs on her, I'm sending in the cavalry.*

What in the heck? I shake my head at him without meaning to.

I bear hard into his eyes, trying to pull something else out of him.

He's so close to confessing. That is, if he did this.

"I'll tell her to expect you," I say. "So, who do you think did this?"

He glances away a moment as if he were considering his

options. *I'm not implicating Nessa. There's no point. She's too close. They work together. She'll want to see the best in her.*

Carter takes a deep breath. "Scout had a pretty clear vendetta against her."

"I heard. Nessa told me about their rivalry. But would she kill over something like that?"

He swills the glass in his hand and the brown liquid nearly sloshes right out.

"Scout would kill. There was a little more to the story than just a few extra fans showing for an event. Yes, Shelby and Chelsea effectively chased her out of the influencer game, but it went a little darker than that." He leans in, his evergreen eyes bearing hard into mine. "Don't believe everything you hear." He pulls a tight smile. "It was nice seeing you."

I watch as he melts into the crowd.

Jasper reappears. His dark brows form a near uniform line across his forehead and it looks strangely sexy.

"Bizzy Baker." He steps in front of me and rocks back on his heels. "You cashed in on that moment of solitude, didn't you?"

My teeth graze my lower lip. "Are you accusing me of nefarious behavior, Detective?"

His cheek rises on one side. "Only because I know you're capable of it."

Jasper pulls me in by the waist and I give his tie a gentle tug.

A dark laugh brews in my chest. "You haven't seen anything yet." Camila runs through my mind. "On second thought, maybe have that conversation with your ex first. She's gunning for you hard, Jasper. And something tells me she won't stop anytime soon."

He glowers out at the crowd.

She's right. If she knew what just happened in the parking lot, she wouldn't feel so generous toward Camila. But then, Bizzy is a good person. She just might despite the fact.

"I'll do it. I'll schedule a sit-down—at the inn. Nothing intimate. I'll let her know that I've moved on and that I don't want any more waves. And, I'll hear her out."

I blow out a breath. "Any chance of reconciling with Leo?" I don't know why I felt the need to ask, but a part of me wanted to. Whether I like it or not, Leo Granger is, well, for lack of a better word, special. And I foresee that he will be in my life in some facet for the unforeseeable future.

Why would she ask about Leo? Of course. That's what he's been doing around her, moping. Making me look like the bad guy. Priming her for the kill before he pounces.

Jasper nods. "I'll have a talk with him, all right." His lips pull back. "But I don't want to talk about Leo. Or the case." There's a pleading look in his eyes. "Let me handle this one, Bizzy." I press my lips tight and offer a meager nod. "Good." Jasper runs his finger over my cheek. "How about we stroll around the exhibit and check out the nudes?" His brows bounce. "In the name of art."

"I've always been a big fan of art."

Jasper and I do just that.

And it feels every bit like a real date.

Of course, I'll let him handle the case—as soon as I have a little talk with Scout Pratt.

CHAPTER 9

"*Y*ou've almost got it." Emmie gives an apprehensive smile as we stare down at the batch of botched pumpkin mini muffins I tried so desperately to bake.

"No, I haven't," I say, chucking the charred treats straight into the trash. "They were burnt *and* undercooked."

Emmie laughs as she pulls me into a tight embrace. "Now that takes a talent. See? You do have talent in the kitchen."

"You're very funny," I say just as I notice a couple of familiar faces stepping up to the counter at the Cottage Café. "My mother and Georgie are here. And I'm pretty sure they won't want anything I dared to put in an oven."

We head up front to where the café is bustling. Just past the patio I can see a bevy of storm clouds on the horizon. The ocean looks dark and angry with navy swells and white caps peppered throughout.

"What can I help you with, ladies?" I ask as they belly up to the register.

Mom looks chic in her bright orange sweater, a black and white checkered collar peeking out from underneath that spikes up to her ears. But her eyes are red with dark rings beneath them and she's pale in general.

"Mom, are you okay?"

"I'm fine." She waves it off. "I just need caffeine. Lots and lots of caffeine. Coffee. Black for me. And throw on a few of those mini muffins. Lord knows I could use some sugar to wake me up, too."

Georgie growls out a laugh. "Your mama had an all-nighter."

Mom is quick to swat her. "Is nothing sacred with you?" Mom shakes her head, her eyes struggling to stay open. "I did not have an all-nighter. Max drove me home and stayed for a drink." She scowls at Georgie. "And that, my friend, is how you say it."

"*Eww?*" I shrug at the thought. "What can I get for you, Georgie?"

"The usual. Bacon and eggs over *greasy*." She gives a greasy wink to match. "Two slices of garlic buttered sourdough—oh, and throw on some biscuits and gravy. And what the heck—load me up with some of those mini muffins as well. I've got a lot of work ahead of me today. I'm all done tracing out my mural. It's time to get glass to concrete." She slaps her hands together and rubs them raw, looking every bit eager—and slightly deranged in the process.

Mom scoffs. "With that meal you'll get things going, all right. I hope the city provided a nice, cushy toilet for you with some decent plumbing."

Georgie waves her off. "The park is just down the street, and while I'm there I get to feed the pigeons, play with the stray cats, and rummage through all those overgrown dumpsters looking for more glass bottles."

Mom closes her eyes like she might be sick. "Sounds like you're living the dream."

"Well, I'm so happy for you, Georgie," I say with a sigh. "I just love seeing you shine."

Georgie is quick to slap Mom on the shoulder. "Your mother was shining, too. Right up until three in the morning."

"Three?" Emmie squeals it out for me. "No wonder you look like death." She winces. "No offense."

Mom lifts a finger. "No offense taken. I've never been put off by the truth. I might be put off by another three in the morning tryst. I really need to build my stamina."

They take off for a booth near the window just as a handsome homicide detective strides on in with his happy-go-lucky pooch by his side.

Emmie leans my way. "I'll get the orders together and take over the register." She gives a sly wink before walking to the kitchen.

"Detective"—I bat my lashes at him playfully—"Sherlock. A big breakfast for you both this morning?"

Jasper looks alarmingly handsome with his hair still glossy from the shower, a black wool coat and jeans. Several of the female customers crane their necks to get a better look at him and I can't blame them. At the moment I'm doing the same.

"Morning, Bizzy." Jasper's eyes are bright as the sun. "Just coffee for me."

And bacon! Sherlock jumps in an effort to see me better. *Bacon, please! Bacon, bacon!*

It takes me less than a minute to get both their orders together.

Jasper nods to the patio. "Would you have a minute to head out for a short walk?"

"For you, I'd carve out all day." I grab my coat and we head out to the briny chilled air. The cove itself curves up against the sandy shores of the inn as if it were giving it a hug. To the left, there's an embankment of boulders, and just beyond that the woods butt right up against the sea. Water might be one of my biggest phobias, but I'm fine with it as long as I'm not in it.

Jasper and I walk out past the cobbled path and head straight into the sand. Fish bounds over and leaps in Sherlock's path, inspiring Jasper to unleash him so the happy pooch can give proper chase.

"And there they go," he says, taking up my hand and landing a soft kiss to my lips. His lids are heavy and there's a slight lazy grin he's slow to part with. "I think we should look into carving out some alone time ourselves."

"We should. Rumor has it, you get a little wild yourself when let off your leash."

A naughty laugh gurgles from his chest. "That's one rumor you should put to the test yourself."

"How does tonight look?"

"I'll be working late. I've got a meeting with the forensics team in a couple of hours and I still have a mound of paperwork on each of the suspects."

"Suspects? Who are you looking at?"

His chest expands. "Bizzy." He winces. "Who are you looking at?" He takes a careful sip of his coffee, those silver eyes never leaving mine.

A laugh bubbles from me. "Okay, fine. I'll give. I don't have any single hard suspect because they're all hard suspects. Jasper, I've never seen so many people who could have easily done this. Is that how most of your investigations work?"

"No, and I'm glad about it. I've had a few cases where it could have been plausible that more than one person pulled the trigger. But, in the end, the evidence always winnows it down to the killer."

"Well, I have to say I'm envious of your exciting job. You must love getting up to go to work in the morning. I mean, it has to be rewarding to put away a killer."

He grins wide for a moment. "It is. But it's tough. You're dealing with a victim—a family who cared about them very much. Believe me when I say this. I envy you, Bizzy. Look at this place." He nods toward the waterline. "You have this majesty right outside your back door. The Country Cottage Inn is a virtual paradise. I may never leave."

My stomach squeezes tight because, in all honesty, I never thought of Jasper leaving, and the idea sends a thin rail of panic in me.

"Well, I'm thrilled to hear you like it here so much."

Fish and Sherlock zoom past us in the opposite direction. Fish is scampering and hopping like a bunny, and Sherlock is bounding like a greyhound at the track.

"So lay out your suspects, Bizzy. Let's see where you are." He gives my hand a quick squeeze.

"There's Chelsea," I volunteer. "She said Shelby did something to her, but she wouldn't say what. She mentioned that Shelby swore her to secrecy while she was alive, and now that she's dead, she's afraid if she tells anyone people will think that not only is she trying to save face, but that it would somehow tarnish Shelby's reputation."

"That's cryptic." Jasper's gaze darts out to the horizon. "I think I need to dig and find out exactly what that could be. Sounds like it has the potential to be a strong motive for murder."

"Well, for what it's worth, she assured me she didn't do it. She did point me toward Carter O'Riley. She basically accused him of being obsessed with Shelby. And from what I gathered last night, that might be the case."

"Did he say anything to implicate himself?"

"Nope. But he did cast suspicion on Scout Pratt. He mentioned that whole fiasco with the Mason jars wasn't all there was to that hazing incident Shelby and Chelsea put her through. He said there was a darker layer to the story. I'm anxious to find out what that could be."

Jasper catches my gaze as we head down to where the sand is damp and easier to walk on.

"Believe me, Bizzy. I will find out and I will tell you in an effort to curb your curiosity. No need to investigate further."

"Well, I wasn't investigating." Was I? "I mean—it wasn't my fault they were simply spilling all they knew. It was just a little friendly chitchat."

Jasper lifts his chin, and that look on his face lets me know he's not buying it.

"Fine." I say, kicking up a little sand. "I may have been investigating, but only because it happened right here at the inn. Anything that concerns the inn concerns me. So where were we?"

"Carter."

"Ah, yes. Anything on him?"

"Did you know he dated Nessa briefly and that's how he met Shelby?"

My mouth falls open. "No, I didn't know that. Although, that would explain why he said he was calling out the cavalry to help get Nessa free. Maybe he still has feelings for her?" Okay, so Carter didn't come right out and say it, but for the sake of Jasper's sanity, we'll say he did.

Jasper's brows hike. "She does have a good defense team lined up. That's very nice of him."

"That is nice. He obviously believes in her innocence. And aside from pointing the finger at Scout, Carter did talk a little about Luke. He said something about Luke being an auto mechanic when he met Shelby, and now he's running a finance department at her father's firm. I thought that was a bit drastic. No real motive for murder."

The night of the slaying flits through my mind. "Wait a minute. I distinctly remember Luke wanting to speak with Shelby, and she was openly giving him the cold shoulder. I think Chelsea mentioned they had just broken up that night. Maybe he killed her because of it?"

"I don't know. But I do need to speak with him further about his relationship with her. He might have had the motive to do it, but motives don't always lead to murder, so you can see where things like forensics come into play."

"Any word on Nessa's gun?" I'm almost sorry I asked. I can't prove that Nessa didn't kill Shelby, but I'd stake my life on it.

"That's exactly what the meeting is about this afternoon." Jasper's mood suddenly sours. "I hope you'll be at peace with whatever we come up with."

"Just because Nessa's gun was used doesn't mean she's the killer."

"It doesn't mean she isn't."

I pause for a moment.

"Have it your way, Detective. But I'll bet you Nessa Crosby had nothing to do with it."

"A bet?"

I offer a confident nod. "Name it. I'll win."

"How about loser has to have the winner over for takeout?"

"That's destined to happen anyways." I rock my shoulder to his.

"Then it sounds like a win-win situation."

I pull him in and a laugh tickles my throat. "It will be. For me." I glance back toward the café and spot my mother and Georgie getting up to leave. "Can you believe my mother and your *brother*? He's the reason she's so exhausted, by the way."

"What can I say—Wilder men have very good taste in women." He pulls back with a mischievous look in his eyes.

"What is it?"

"All right. I'll tell you, but if word gets around, I'll deny I ever said it."

I give his ribs a quick pinch and he bucks with a laugh.

"I give." He holds up a hand briefly. "I might have another brother who is a bit exhausted today because he spent last night at the hands of a Baker woman."

My eyes widen in horror as I quickly do the Baker woman math and gasp.

Jasper lands a finger to my lips and shakes his head. "It's okay. He was more than a willing participant."

"But—"

Jasper lands a heated kiss right over my lips, and it warms me from the inside out.

Something tells me I've already won with Jasper.

All I have to do now is clear Nessa's name.

And I'm about to spend the rest of my day doing exactly that.

Right after I hunt down that wily Baker woman.

CHAPTER 10

The sun breaks out through the cloud cover, shining all of its autumn glory over the Haunted Harvest Festival fairgrounds—and the Montgomerys have their farm set up in exactly that way.

This week's newest addition is a series of tents where local businesses and crafters showcase their wares. And it just so happens to be where I was able to track down a certain quasi-celebrity author and her underling—Ginger King and Scout Pratt.

And knowing that Ginger would be here is the exact reason I decided to bring Peanut along. The tiny black and white puppy leaps and skips with unmitigated joy as he takes in the farm. Okay, so maybe I didn't exactly tell him we would be bumping into Ginger, but he doesn't have to worry regardless. There's no way I'm letting anything happen to him—and he is definitely coming home with me.

I could live here, Bizzy. I love the great outdoors. There's nothing like a little sunshine on my back to make me feel young again.

A tiny laugh bumps through me. "Peanut, you are a puppy," I say, giving his leash a playful tug.

I haven't just brought Peanut along for the ride, I brought my wild-for-the-Wilders sister along as well.

Macy and I hit the hot apple cider booth before we head toward the craft booths and I take a careful sip of my cider before examining my spicy sister. Her blonde hair is stick straight, hitched back behind her ears, and she and I have inadvertently donned matching yellow and black flannels, worn jeans, and cute little suede booties. She's already pointed out that we're double the trouble, double the fun.

"How could you sleep with Dalton?" I ask and watch with a smidge of delight as she chokes and gags on her very next sip.

Her eyes widen. "Just cut to the bone, why don't you."

"That's the only way to do things with you, and we both know it." True as gospel.

"Calm down, Grandma Bizzy. It was no big deal." Macy makes a face as she stirs the drink in her hand with a cinnamon stick.

"Excuse me? Staying the night is a *very* big deal. He's going to think you're easy."

"I *am* easy." She inches back. "Have you met me?"

"Unfortunately."

"And before you go spreading rumors to Mom, it wasn't Dalton. And he didn't spend the night. It was Jamison, and I slapped him silly until he limped out of my place around three a.m."

My mouth falls open. "So you chose the attorney? And what is it with you and Mom at three a.m.? It's like the witching hour with the two of you."

"That's for me to know and you to find out. And when are you and Jasper going to lock yourselves in a room until three in the morning? You're falling woefully behind. Time's a tickin'."

My cheeks burn with heat at the thought.

"I don't know." I scowl out at the burgeoning crowd. "I told him to talk it out with his ex before we took things further. We're not even in a real commitment yet."

Macy scoffs. "So what? I'm definitely not in a real commitment." Her phone chirps and she laughs like a woodpecker as she reads the text. "Jamison is coming by tonight at eight. He's got a long day at the office, but he's bringing takeout." She sings that last bit.

"Takeout?" I give a wistful shake of the head. "Rumor has it, sharing late night Chinese is the road to a solid commitment. You're moving awful fast, you know."

"That's because I haven't done anything stupid like asking him to hash things out with his ex. Maybe you really do need a copy of Ginger King's book on how to snag a man. Did you take notes during that seminar? Mom and I were riveted students and we've already netted a Wilder apiece."

"To be fair, she had one in the hand going in. And please refrain from joking about what she might be holding. I can only take so much."

We come upon the craft booths that sit under a massive tent with a sign up above that reads *Happy Falloween!* and I quickly spot a small crowd around Ginger. Scout isn't anywhere to be seen at the moment, but Nessa assured me they were both here. It was Nessa whom I enlisted to help track them down. Of course, I didn't mention that it was her hide I was looking to save.

I pick up Peanut, and once he spots Ginger, his entire body goes rigid.

No, Bizzy, no! I'll do anything not to go with her again. I promise I'll stop nipping at Sherlock's tail. I'll even stop sneaking bites of Fish's Fancy Beast cat food. Just let me live, Bizzy. Let me live!

I tuck a quick kiss between his ears. "I promise that no matter what happens, you're coming right back home with me today. You were her link to Shelby. You might elicit some incriminating thoughts. I just want to see how she'll respond to you."

Peanut whimpers and hides his face in my flannel. *She'll eat me is how she'll respond. She's already licking her lips, readying for her afternoon snack.*

"That's because you look adorably delicious."

Macy leans in. "Stop talking to the dog and tell me what you want me to do."

"I don't know. Tell her you're here looking into renting a booth for Lather and Light? Come to think of it, why aren't you renting a booth for your shop? This would be perfect for you."

Macy grunts, "Because then I would actually have to show up and work. Not all of us have an inn we can ignore, Bizzy." She threads her arm through mine as we stride boldly in Ginger's direction.

I make a face. "You do realize what you just said makes zero sense."

"Only to you, my sweet little sister. Only to you. Now, if you could stay up partying with a Wilder boy until the wee hours of the morning like your mother and me—you'd be far more enlightened."

Peanut squirms in my arms. *That's a great idea, Bizzy. If you played more with Jasper at night, I could play more with Sherlock. Fish doesn't care for games as much as he does.*

"I'll keep that in mind," I say as I seriously consider taking one for the team.

We step into the booth just as the small crowd disperses.

Ginger does a quick double take at the cute puppy in my arms and her eyes widen, and her expression turns to stone before she jumps to her feet. Her red hair is wild in loose waves, and she's heavily dusted her eyelids with bright green frosted eye shadow. She's pretty, stunningly so, and yet there's a slight plastic element about her overall that I can't quite put my finger on.

"Hey, I recognize you." She snaps her finger in my direction.

"I'm the manager at the Country Cottage Inn, and this is my sister, Macy."

Macy leans in. "I'm looking into a booth for her shop. I mean, *my* shop. The one I hate to love. I mean, love to hate." She tosses her hand in the air. "I really just need a copy of your book for my sister. She's got a good man, but she keeps trying to give him away."

Ginger laughs. "Help yourself. In fact, I'll gift you both a copy."

"Great." Macy takes off to peruse the merchandise on the shelves set up in the back.

Ginger twists her lips while looking at Peanut. "Funny—I haven't missed you."

Peanut glances my way. *At least she doesn't mince words.*

"Don't worry," I'm quick to tell her. "Peanut is welcome to stay with me as long as he needs to. Do you happen to know if Shelby has any family asking about him?"

He whines and buries his face in my flannel once again.

"Nope." Ginger digs her fists into her hips. "The little twerp is all yours for the taking. So, have they arrested Nessa yet?"

My eyes flash to hers.

Great. She shoots a quick glance out at the crowd. *She probably wonders how I know about Nessa.*

Ginger leans in. "It's no secret Nessa was out to get her. In fact, we all heard her threaten Shelby just minutes before she died."

"I know," I say it low. "So, is that who you think did it?"

Her glossy pink lips twist in a knot. "I'm positive Nessa did it. I'd bet money on it anyway."

Poor Nessa. If this went to Vegas, I have a feeling the odds would be against her.

Ginger rides her eyes over me as if sizing me up. *She's too close to Nessa to think anything bad about her.*

She frowns my way. "You don't think Nessa did it." She shakes her head. "I get it. She's your subordinate. She does what you tell her and she's gained your trust. But you'll see. This will all come down to Nessa in the end." You can take that all the way to the bank.

I wrinkle my nose without meaning to. "Well, outside of Nessa, who do you think could have done something so terrible?"

Here we go. She folds her arms across her chest.

Peanut perks to life and opens a single eye in her direction. *She's guilty, isn't she, Bizzy? Call Jasper and have him cuff her. I'll be the first to cheer him on.*

A quiet laugh bounces through me.

Ginger gives a quick glance around. "Just between you and me, there was some shady stuff going on between Shelby and Scout."

"*Scout?*" I practically mouth her name.

She nods. "Did Nessa tell you about their dealings?"

"The meet and greet nightmare?"

A dark brow anchors itself far into her forehead. "Is that all you know?"

I give a quick nod, half-afraid I'll spook her if I speak.

Her lips swim with a greedy grin. "That's not all that happened before Shel and Chelsea decided to detonate her influencer career."

"What?"

Gingers nods as she steps in close. "It has to do with Scout's cousin. She's a successful realtor out in Sheffield."

I avert my eyes at the name of the town. That's where Camila hails from and works. That's where Jasper lived before moving to Cider Cove to get away from her.

I lean in. "Why do I get the feeling nothing good happened in Sheffield?"

She tips her head my way. "Because you're intuitive, Bizzy." She crimps her lips. "Before Scout's foray into the deep end of social media, she was working a summer internship for her cousin."

"The realtor." I nod.

"Yup. She did a lot of open houses for her cousin. It's sort of the grunge work in that field. And a lot of those homes were still being lived in. Scout found it creepy standing around in someone else's living room all day with hardly anyone coming by but one or two people. Once, she had a guy show up and she couldn't get him to leave. After that, she didn't feel safe. So, being the sensible girl she is, she started asking her friends to stay with her and the only taker was Shelby." She leans in. "Can you guess how Shelby entertained herself while the two of them were stuck inside a stranger's house for hours at a time?"

I glance over my shoulder just as a row of maple trees rain down their fiery red leaves.

"No," I say, stepping in closer to her. "How?"

"She stole." A satisfied smile cinches across Ginger's face.

"She stole?" My eyes widen in horror.

Ginger gives a hearty nod. "Mostly jewelry. Small trinkets no one would suspect were missing right away. Shelby told me they found some money tucked in the back of a closet once. Stole that wad of cash, too. Shelby didn't need it, of course. It was the thrill of it all. But it gave her something other than a thrill." She hikes a shoulder my way. "*Control*. She had Scout in her back pocket."

I shake my head as I try to wrap my mind around it. "That's terrible. And why did she want to control Scout to begin with?"

"Who didn't she want to control? All Shelby's life she didn't have a say in anything. Her parents made sure she was well taken care of, but she didn't have a say in the details of her life, the minutia. I guess you could chalk it up to a poor little rich girl crisis. And Shelby seemed to have every crisis known to man. But as far as controlling Scout, let's just say she was her pet project. Eventually, though, Scout was confronted by her cousin about the thefts. She thought it was an awful coincidence that every house Scout was assigned to was reporting a robbery. When push came to shove, Scout ratted Shelby out. Scout's cousin threatened to call the police. Of course, Shelby put that fire out right away.

She made it clear that she would find a way to ruin her if she did, and she made an example of Scout to be sure she got the message."

My mouth falls open. "And that's why she pulled that stunt with her followers? Wow, she was cunning."

Peanut cowers and nuzzles close. *I can't listen to this anymore. Wake me when it's over.*

"She *was* cunning," Ginger agrees. "Book smart, too." Her eyes harden as she gazes back out at the crowds. *And that's exactly why I needed her.*

I blink over at her. "And what was your relationship with Shelby like?"

Ginger takes a quick breath. "That little beast in your hand was about the extent of it. Scout thought it would be good PR to have something to soften me. She thinks I'm a little rough around the edges. Personally, I think people respect that. More importantly, *men* respect that." She leans in, her hand pressed to her chest. "Speaking of which, did you happen to catch a glimpse of that hot homicide detective? That boy can do a full body search on me anytime he wishes." A sultry laugh gurgles from her. "Don't say a word, but I'm planning to stop by the Seaview Sheriff's Department sometime this week with the pretense of checking up on the case." She jolts back. "Hey? The inn baked those fabulous pumpkin muffins, right? I might stop by and pick up a dozen or so and take them with me. Everyone knows the true blue way to a man's heart is through his stomach."

"I'll keep that in mind." It takes everything in me not to scowl at her.

A girl staggers in next to me and we turn to find Scout with her arms laden down with cups of steaming cider, a couple of churros, and a funnel cake.

"I got all the food you wanted, Ginger." She does a double take in my direction. "Hey!" She gives an easy smile. "You're the girl from the inn. Nessa's friend, right?"

"That's me. My sister is looking into getting a booth here at the festival."

Macy clears her throat. "I'm looking to help my sister land a man. A little honesty goes a long way, Bizzy. And men happen to like it."

Ginger laughs. "Only on occasion." She winks my way. "I'll go sign those books for you."

She takes off and Scout heads my way. "Any word on who could have done this?" She gives Peanut a quick scratch between the ears and he slowly lifts his head out of his slumber. Peanut, by far, is the easiest dog to take care of.

"Not yet. But I hear the sheriff's department is running a forensic test on some evidence they found." I shrug. "I'm not sure what, though." I'm not about to sell the farm.

Scout's mouth rounds out as she glances to Ginger. *So they must know.*

A breath hitches in my throat. What must they know? That it was Nessa's gun? Or that Scout herself had reason enough to kill.

She offers a weak smile my way. "Any word on when they'll be making an arrest?" She swallows hard, and I can't help but think she's looking guilty.

"No. I don't have any idea if they're at that point yet."

Poor Nessa. She shakes her head as she glances back to Ginger. *She will never know what hit her.*

My stomach churns just hearing it. Another strike for Nessa. But in my heart, I can't seem to agree with any of them.

Macy and I collect our signed copies and thank Ginger profusely. We say goodbye to the two of them and filter our way back into the crowd with Peanut still cradled in my arms.

And all the way back to the inn, those cryptic words ring out in my mind.

Poor Nessa.

CHAPTER 11

Once or twice a season, my mother and Georgie will unite unlikely forces in the ballroom right here at the inn and host an afternoon craft festival of their own. The two of them each bring the supplies for a relatively easy craft—and any and every guest of the inn is invited to participate. Judging by the turnout, most have decided to do just that. Even Gwyneth and Camila have joined the ranks of the crafty this morning. Not that it should surprise me. They already have the cunning part down pat.

I head into the ballroom and set down another couple of platters of the café's pumpkin spice mini muffins. I do a quick inspection of the hot apple cider carafes to make sure the refreshment table is amply supplied, and all is well on that front.

Georgie has everyone making adorable pumpkins made out of old flannels she picked up at the secondhand store, and a brand new roll of toilet paper. Yes, toilet paper.

And my mother has bought out all the orange burlap in the land, along with wire wreath frames and has the other half of the room fashioning together gorgeous fall wreaths. There's just a smidge of green burlap up top to make it look like a pumpkin.

At least both Mom and Georgie are sticking to a theme.

I'm about to make my way over to them when Camila lets out a sharp cackle.

"I certainly hope so," she says to Gwyneth, loud enough for everyone in the vicinity to hear, so I decide to rearrange the napkins in the event she wants to extrapolate on that little tidbit. "It's been so long since I've shared a meal with your son. I can hardly wait for tonight."

Tonight? Which son? My goodness, is she talking about dinner with Jasper?

Gwyneth sighs. "I'll be sure to make an early departure. I've arranged for a date to meet me there. As soon as I spot him, I'll bolt. The two of you really need to have some good one-on-one time together."

One-on-one? As in a date of their own?

My blood boils at the thought of it. Jasper just mentioned that he wanted to spend more time with *me*. Clearly, going to dinner with Camila is a step backward in the endeavor.

Camila pauses from her wreath-making a moment and glances my way, inspiring me to spin back around to the refreshment table and pour myself a cup of cider.

I don't see why not. There's plenty enough for me to drown my sorrows with.

"I wonder what he wants to speak with me about?" she says it a notch quieter, for Gwyneth's ears only.

I suck in a quick breath. Wait a minute. *Talk* to her?

Hey? Wait a minute. That was my bright idea.

Gwyneth laughs. "Oh, my dear, that's just an old ploy to get you alone. Once you're together, that old spark will reignite. Be sure to dress to enchant. Don't waste a single moment while trying to get back in his good graces. He is a man, after all. They respond to one thing and one thing only."

One thing? Good grief. Why do I get the feeling good old

Gwyneth is rooting for Camila and Jasper to join the three a.m. club?

They share a laugh because, apparently, they can now read my mind, too.

The room breaks out into a collective coo as if a litter of kittens had just emerged from all that burlap my mother is trying to wrap the world in, and I turn to find Nessa smiling as she takes Peanut for a lap through the crowd.

I'll admit, he is show-stoppingly cute.

I stop playing with the napkins and meet her halfway.

"Good work," I say as I bend over and give Peanut a scratch on the head.

Nessa gave me bacon. He wags his little stumpy tail. *She said if I'm extra nice I'll get another piece, too! I like pieces of bacon, Bizzy. And I need all the pieces I can get.*

I can't help but laugh as I straighten. "Do I sense a bacon bribe?" I say to Nessa and she rolls her eyes.

"I swear, Bizzy, sometimes I think you have a sixth sense." *Good thing she can't read minds. I think I'd be toast if anyone could.*

I frown over at her. The last thing I want to hear either verbally or otherwise is a confession coming from her.

"Is everything okay, Nessa?"

"As okay as it can be. Grady is watching the desk, so I thought I'd make the rounds with this adorable creature."

"No problem. I think it's good for both Peanut and the guests. Poor thing needs all the love the world can shower him with."

"Oh, I plan on showering him with all my affection." Nessa watches as a couple of women dote over him. "In fact, if he needs a good home, I'd be happy to keep him. I'd spoil that baby boy rotten."

Peanut stops short and quickly traipses over.

Oh, Bizzy, can she keep me? Can she? Can she?

"I think someone understood exactly what you said." I laugh.

"I don't see why not. No one has come forth to claim him. And Ginger is the last person I would have let take him."

He whines at the mention of her name.

Nessa squeals with delight. "Really? I'm going straight to Pet World after work to pick up a dog bed and those cute little ceramic dishes with paw prints all over them. And, oh, some toys! Lots and lots of toys."

Peanut dances in a spastic circle. His thoughts are on overload as he basks in the joy.

"It's a match made in Country Cottage Inn heaven," I say as we part ways and I head over to the double trouble stationed at the head of the room.

"Ladies," I say to both my mother and Georgie. "I'm in love with both of these ideas. The two of you really are creative. Can I get ten of these to go?" I say to Georgie, holding up an adorable red and black flannel pumpkin.

Mom scoffs. "I hear they really come in handy if you keep them in the bathroom."

Georgie waves her off. "Oh, you. And I hear your burlap really comes in handy if you need to tie up an intruder. Speaking of strange men roving into your home at all hours of the night..." She elbows my mother in the ribs. "You still entertaining a certain gentleman caller?"

Mom glances my way. Her blue eyes brighten her face a notch, and I can't help but note she has a dewy youthful glow about her.

"Maybe. Maybe not." She makes a face. "I think I'm too old for this booty call business."

"*Eww.*" I inch back. "TMI—as in too much information? Is that all he wants from you?"

"Well, no. I mean, I invite him in for a drink and, of course, we talk. But then, one drink leads to much more aerobic activity that happens to last well into the wee hours of the morning." She tosses a mound of orange burlap to the table in front of her.

"How do I tell my thirty-something boyfriend that I prefer to be in bed by eight? I'm not sure how much longer I can keep up with him. The man has boundless energy. He cooks in the restaurant all day and—"

Georgie lifts a finger. "He cooks in the bedroom all night."

"And this is where I leave you." A laugh percolates in my chest. "Good job, ladies," I say as I head for the entrance, but a certain deputy speaking to Camila stops me dead in my tracks. It's Leo.

He glances my way. *Hello, Bizzy.*

I nod over to him. *Hey, Leo. Rekindling an old flame? I'll be the last to stop you.*

Camila follows his gaze and frowns. *I bet she'd love to see me run back to this one. Sorry, Dizzy. One of us doesn't get what she wants in this equation, and that one would be you.*

I avert my eyes as I head for the lobby, and Leo follows me right out the door.

"Bizzy?"

I pause as he heads my way. "It sounds as if Camila is set to give you a run for your money."

A dull laugh pumps through my chest. "I try not to let myself be ruled by aggression or fear." *Camila just so happens to dole out both.*

He laughs. "That she does."

I give a quick glance around. "The other day you were telling me about those who are transmundane. You alluded there were other abilities." It took everything in me not to call them powers.

He nods. "There are at least a handful of other known *powers* that we know about." He gives a bemused smile when he puts the emphasis on the word *powers*, and I cinch a wry smile.

"Boy, I must be an easy read," I say.

He lifts a dark brow. "The pure at heart often are."

"Don't keep me in suspense. What are these powers? How many of us are there?"

Leo's lips part, but his attention is hijacked by something

117

behind me and I turn to see Jasper stalking on over. He looks lean and mean and drop-dead gorgeous in a dangerous way.

"Jasper." I straighten as if I were caught with my hand in the Leo Granger cookie jar.

"Hey, Bizzy." His lips curve, but he's missing a smile. "I'm afraid I'm here on business." He glowers at Leo momentarily.

What's it going to take to keep this guy away from her? Every time I turn around, he's doing his best to lock her into a conversation. And to think I entertained the idea of letting bygones be bygones. It's clear Leo is still gunning to eviscerate me. I will never understand what happened between us. We were closer than brothers. It was as if he always knew what I was thinking.

I'm tempted to swat Leo, but decide to hold back for now. Of course, Jasper thought that. It was true.

It was. And I did care about him like a brother. Leo nods to Jasper. *Still do. I'll find a way to fix things. I just don't know how or when.*

I clear my throat as I look to Jasper. "You're here on business? What kind of business?" I run my finger down his tie absent-mindedly and something in me heats. Okay, fine. I'll admit, that conversation about my mother's late night hookups has my hormones cruising in all kinds of interesting directions. A small part of me thinks the only Baker woman who should be indulging in a Wilder man is *me*.

It's wrong, I know.

I take a moment to shoot Leo a look because I happen to know he heard and he bounces his brows as if to affirm this.

"I'm sorry, Bizzy." Jasper pulls me in and wraps his arms around me momentarily. "I'm here for Nessa."

"Nessa?"

No sooner does he say her name than Peanut bounces by with Nessa laughing along.

"Just as I suspected"—she pauses next to us and Peanut hops

backward—"the little guy was a hit. I think I'll take him to the café for that treat I promised him."

Bacon, bacon, bacon. Peanut spins in a circle as if he were crazed.

"Nessa"—Jasper's chest expands as he steps to the side—"I'm afraid I'm going to have to bring you down to the Seaview Sheriff's Department for more questioning."

"Why?" Her eyes bulge, and her tawny skin lights up bright pink from the shock of it.

"Forensics came back. The bullet that killed Shelby Harris was a match."

"Oh my goodness." Nessa presses her hand to her chest. "But we knew that." She shakes her head vigorously. "I already told you—someone fired my gun. But it wasn't me."

Jasper closes his eyes for a moment. "I know we covered that, but a witness has stepped forward."

"A *witness?*" both Nessa and I sing it out like a choir.

Jasper nods. "And he has informed us that you were having a full-fledged argument with Shelby in the courtyard where she was killed."

"I"—Nessa gives me a nervous glance—"It's true, but it's not what it seems."

"He said it got physical."

"She pushed me." Nessa shakes her head in horror. "Bizzy, you have to believe me. I didn't do this. I'm not going to Seaview. I'm not going to prison for something I didn't do!"

Jasper's lips harden, but his eyes are full of sympathy for the poor girl.

"I'm sorry, Nessa. You'll have to come with me." He glances my way. "I'm sorry."

Jasper carefully navigates a panicked Nessa to the door as Peanut runs in a circle around my feet and I quickly pick him up.

Go save her, Bizzy! Go get my Nessa!

"I wish I could," I say, dotting his fur with a kiss.

Peanut whimpers in her wake. *I'd give all the bacon in the world to save her.*

My arms tighten around the sweet angel.

Leo takes a breath. "She sure sounds convincingly innocent. But then, most of them do."

"Well, she *is*," I say it with only half the conviction I once had. I suppose everyone is capable of a dark moment or two in their lives. "I'm going to use my powers for good, Leo. I'm going to find out who really killed Shelby Harris." My heart pumps wildly at the thought of what I'm about to say next. "And I want you to help me."

CHAPTER 12

*N*essa was arrested.

Arrested.

I can't seem to wrap my head around this. Her family is down at the Seaview Sheriff's Department right now trying to convince anyone who will listen that she's innocent—but now I'm beginning to wonder about Nessa's innocence myself.

Nessa's older sister, Vera, is furious at *me* of all people. And the rumor mill—that would be Emmie—has it that Vera is plotting her vengeance against yours truly.

My phone pings and it's a text from Jasper.

How about dinner?

I wrinkle my nose at the screen. I hardly have an appetite after the news with Nessa. A thought comes to me and I text him back. **Are you sure you're free for dinner?**

I hate to be the one to remind him about his quasi-date with his ex, but I'm not looking for any more drama today.

My phone lights up again with another text from Jasper. **Shoot. I just remembered I told my mother I'd have dinner with her. Please join us. My mind has been all over the place today. I could really use your company.**

Ugh. His mother? That's right. The big scheme I overheard her dreaming up. Who knows, maybe I'll get lucky and Camila will cancel.

Far be it from me to turn the offer down, so I put on my little black dress, my fancy houndstooth black and white coat—a discard of Macy's—and my long, black, suede boots that look as if they have their own naughty intentions.

Jasper brings Sherlock over to my place so he can hang out with both Fish and Peanut and we take off to a restaurant called A Fork in the Road. It's an Italian-Asian fusion restaurant that I'm not entirely sure knows how it feels about itself. Yes, I said that correctly.

A Fork in the Road has been sitting on the distal tip of Main Street for a couple of years now, but for some reason, I've never ventured past its doors.

Inside, it's dimly lit. The sound of exotic twanging instruments filters through the speakers, and the hushed whispers of the patrons just beyond the foyer sounds like the undercurrent of excitement that only a Friday night can bring.

"Bizzy." Jasper pulls me to the side a moment. That wicked half-smile on his face lets me know he's hungry for far more than food. "You look amazing tonight."

My cheeks heat. "You may have mentioned it a time or two, but I'm not going to stop you anytime soon." I hike up on my tiptoes, land a kiss to his lips, and make it linger. "Thank you, by the way."

A dull growl works its way up his throat. "I say we eat and run."

"What? No dessert? That's practically sacrilegious." I blink up at him, not minding at all that I'm openly flirting.

"We'll pick up donuts on the way home. Or better yet, we'll raid the café. Those pumpkin spice mini muffins are to die for."

I twist my lips. "No dying allowed tonight." I crane my neck past him. "We'd better not keep your mother waiting. I don't think she's that impressed with me."

Jasper leans back. "What are you talking about? My mother loves you. Or at least she will once she gets to know you. She's just a little stressed dealing with the flooding in her townhouse. It looks as if she's going to have to move."

"Oh, that is terrible. Of course, she's dealing with a lot. I feel horrible for saying that. I promise I wasn't trying to make it all about me."

A dull laugh thumps through him. "Believe me when I say I want to focus on you alone. Let's get going."

Jasper spots his mother, already seated, and begins to navigate us in that direction when I sense a disturbance in the force. It's an odd feeling I get whenever something negative is about to—

"Bizzy?" a male voice calls out.

I turn to my right and suck in a quick breath. It's Leo Granger seated directly across from Mack Woods.

Oh my Lord up in heaven, now this is a pairing if ever there was one.

I glance up ahead, and I've momentarily lost Jasper in the crowded restaurant.

"Wow," I say, still trying to wrap my head around the scene. "Mayor Woods, Leo." I shoot him a bemused smile. *You have a propensity for barracudas, I see.*

His eyes widen a notch. *That bad, huh?*

Worse. I smile over at Mack, but she's not smiling back.

Jasper appears and says a quick hello. "Mayor Woods." He nods her way.

Mack looks cuttingly sharp tonight with her dark red lips and eyes lined like an Egyptian pharaoh.

"Detective." Her smile broadens. *Now there's a piece of meat I'd like to take a bite out of.*

I can't help but lift a brow at Leo. As much as I'm trying not to say *I told you so*, I think there's an entire choir of that very phrase going off in my mind.

Leo shakes his head as if it weren't a big deal.

The man must have an ego made of steel.

"Any word on our killer?" Mack addresses the question to Jasper.

He expands his chest. "We made an arrest. Nessa Crosby. Things moved very quickly after forensics came back with hard evidence."

We've yet to discuss this so-called "hard evidence". I didn't want to pull us down that rabbit hole once he picked me up for our date. But as soon as we get back to my cottage, I'll do a little interrogating myself. And I won't let Jasper leave until I get a complete confession out of him. I've got a few tricks up my sleeve to make sure he tells me everything I want to know.

Mack's mouth falls open. "Nessa?" She looks just as affronted by the arrest as I feel. Mack is good friends with both Vera and Nessa. And for once, I'm glad about the fact she's conned the good people of Cider Cove into giving her so much political power. Maybe she'll put it to good use for once—like pardoning a prisoner. "I always suspected that girl was up to no good."

"*Mack!*" I squawk her name so loud half the restaurant turns in our direction.

Her eyes narrow in on mine. "What's the matter, Bizzy? Are you upset you didn't get to the killer first? Or, let me guess—you were about to give her a free pass just because she works at your silly little inn."

A choking sound emits from my throat. "Silly little inn?"

Jasper offers them both a quick wave as he wraps an arm around my waist.

"Enjoy your dinner," he says. ***The two of you just might deserve each other.***

A tiny laugh bubbles up my throat. Although, I'm not sure if I agree with him entirely. Leo can't be all that bad.

Thank you, Bizzy, Leo says from afar and I turn and shoot a sly smile his way.

Jasper stops short just shy of his mother and I crane my neck trying to look past his shoulder.

"What's going on?"

"Bizzy"—his voice is low and slow—"I promise I had nothing to do with this."

And just like that, my stomach knots up because I have a sneaking suspicion I know exactly what's going on.

Jasper steps over, exposing the exact malfeasance I pegged it to be.

"Mom, Camila." Jasper nods before turning my way. "It looks as if we're going to have a full table."

Camila's mouth rounds out in horror at the sight of me.

How did this happen? She casts a hard look to Gwyneth who offers a circular shrug.

Gwyneth's lips expand my way as if it took all her energy to feign a smile. With her dark hair pulled back, her silver eyes flashing, she looks like Jasper in female skin.

This is far more serious than I thought. She cringes openly my way. *Certainly Jasper has had his fair share of floozies. Why this one?* She shakes her head as she openly examines me.

We exchange polite hellos as Jasper pulls my seat out, landing me right next to his mother.

Just perfect.

Camila looks stunning tonight with her hair set in soft waves, a bright red dress that screams *I'm planning to dig my claws into my ex tonight,* and a large sparkler on her ring finger of all places that looks suspiciously like something of an engagement nature.

"Bizzy"—Camila leans in, placing her left hand onto the table in plain view, in the event I missed the quasi-matrimonial stunt— "so nice to see you away from the inn." *The woman is a walking horror story.* "I think you and I will grow to be fast friends." *Or*

125

even faster enemies. "We should plan a girls' day out sometime." *In about fifty years.*

My gaze falls to that sparkler once again.

Has Jasper ever mentioned the fact they were engaged?

Although, they did date for four years. If they weren't engaged by then, it was very patient of Camila to sit around and hope for a ring. That is, if that's what she wanted.

"A girls' day?" I clear my throat. "That would be great." The words strum from me so low I hardly heard them.

She can't even fake being nice to me. Camila frowns my way momentarily. *Most likely because I've stunned her into submission with this rock on my finger. That's right, Bizzy, read the carats and weep.*

Gwyneth takes in a quick breath. "Is that your engagement ring, Camila? My, is it ever stunning. No use in letting that sit around in a drawer." She looks to Jasper and winks. "Good on you for wearing it."

Jasper shifts in his seat. *I would have preferred the drawer. I probably should have taken it back when she offered. Had I known it would be used as ammo to take me down at a later time, I would have demanded it myself.*

I glance over to Jasper and shake my head just a smidge.

He's got it wrong. Camila isn't trying to take him down. She's trying to pull him in.

"Yes, it is." Camila covers the ring for a moment. "I'm afraid I've made it a habit to wear it. My finger just feels naked without it."

Jasper reaches over and picks up my hand. "Bizzy, Camila and I were briefly engaged. It was a month, wasn't it?" He tips his chin down while offering her a look that sears. "That's when you decided that Leo was a better fit for you."

Her eyes flare with rage, and suddenly it looks as if Gwyneth and I are about to be caught in the crosshairs of a lovers' spat. Ironically, the lovers would be my boyfriend and his ex.

My stomach cinches because Jasper and I aren't officially official just yet. And if Camila gets her way, that will never happen.

Camila takes a breath. "Yes, well, that's ancient history now. He's here with another woman. Clearly, he's moved on and so have I. I'm single." Her bone-white teeth graze over her lower lip, a clear invitation if ever there was one.

"I'm taken." Jasper doesn't miss a beat.

But before Camila can gag or evaporate or whatever her splendid response will be, a figure darkens the table and I gasp at the sight.

"Dad?" I nearly eject myself out my seat at the sight of him.

"Bizzy Bizzy." He comes over and plants a kiss to my cheek. My father has wide blue eyes and a boyish charm that has allowed him to get away with everything for as long as he's existed. Although, any one of his vast collection of ex-wives might disagree with me on that—starting with my mother. "Everyone looks happy and healthy." He shakes Jasper's hand before nodding over to Camila. "Gwyneth, have I interrupted your dinner?"

Jasper's mother looks horrified. *How do I leave Camila here with that woman holding onto Jasper as if he were a life raft? Maybe I can coerce her to come along. This is her father, after all. But then, there goes my date. She's just ruining everything tonight.*

Did she say *date*?

Gwyneth's not dating my father, is she?

GAH! Did I do something to seriously offend the universe? If so, I demand to know—and I might demand a recount, too.

I clear my throat. "Dad, why don't you join us?"

"Yes." Jasper quickly grabs a seat from an empty table behind us and adds it to the mix. Soon, a waitress comes by and adds a table setting for him and we all put in our dinner orders.

I catch Camila ogling my father long after the waitress takes off.

He is something. Look at those eyes. And that naughty grin? Now there's a silver fox I wouldn't mind hunting.

"No," I say, looking right at her and she gasps my way.

"Excuse me?" Her expression quickly morphs to annoyance. "Did you say no?"

I take in a quick breath as all eyes feast on me. "I said *oh*. As in, a thought just occurred to me." I look to my father. "Are you meeting someone here? We're not interrupting your date, are we?"

That permanent smile my father wears expands with devious delight. "I was meeting someone here. And it was a date. In fact, the woman in question is seated right next to you."

I curl my lips with satisfaction. If I have to know about our parents' questionable dalliance, Jasper should, too. If Jasper feels as grossed out as I do, we'll be able to squash this budding romance like a cockroach.

Who are we kidding? This is no budding romance. More like a seriously offensive senior moment.

A deep groan comes from Jasper as if he were mortally wounded.

"The two of you were going on a *date?*" His brows hike as he inspects my father first and then his mother.

Dad nods with that wide-eyed charm. Thankfully for him, he was born with a face that no one could really stay mad at.

And Gwyneth looks as if she's the cat who ate the canary.

"Mom?" Jasper shakes his head at the woman who can't seem to contain her devilish grin. "No offense to Nathan, but he has a reputation for being extremely fond of the ladies."

Gwyneth frowns heavily at her son. "I should hope so. I happen to fall in that category. Nathan, please excuse my son. He's a bit overprotective of me."

Jasper grunts as he looks to my father, "And I have two brothers that are just as overprotective."

Camila chortles to herself as she sits back and watches my worst nightmare unfold.

She coos over at him, sparkler front and center. "Jasper is quite protective of those he cares about. That's what I miss about you most." She all but blows him a kiss. "Don't give Gwynie such a hard time. It's nice to know that romance doesn't die once you crest the other side of the hill." She runs her hand along my father's arm and his brows hike up, amused by this young temptress by his side. "And I can see the lure. It's safe to say, Gwyneth, you've managed to snag yourself the stud of the bunch."

Gwyneth goes rigid as she looks to the girl she was so quick to upsell to her son. It looks as if the medicine doesn't go down as easily as she was willing to dole it out.

How do you like that, Gwynie? Camila is trying to simultaneously steal my man *and* yours. Now there's a reality check.

Dad clears his throat, looking slightly uncomfortable for the first time in his life.

"So Jasper?" He leans his way. "Rumor has it, there's been an arrest in the case. Let me guess, disgruntled ex?"

"No, actually." Jasper offers me a silent apology with his eyes. "It was Nessa Crosby."

"Little Nessie?" Dad leans back. "Are you sure about that?"

Jasper ticks his head to the side. "We had an eyewitness come forward that placed her at the scene of the crime. And forensics confirmed it was her weapon that killed the victim."

I catch his eye. "Who was the eyewitness?"

He pauses a moment and glances around the table. *If we were alone, I'd tell her who it was.* "I'm sorry, Bizzy. That's confidential at the moment. But I'm sure it'll all come out in the wash." *Luke was skittish to begin with. I should be the last person whispering his name—especially in front of three other people.*

Luke.

Luke Parker, Shelby's boyfriend.

Actually, that's not right. Chelsea let me know Shelby cut him loose right before she was killed. He placed Nessa at the scene of the crime?

"Bizzy"—Dad interrupts my thoughts—"didn't you grow up with Nessa? She's no killer, is she?"

"Yes and no. I can promise everyone at this table she's not capable of such a thing."

Camila averts her gaze. "Believe me, even the tenderest of souls can be driven to the brink of madness." *I should know. I'm almost there myself. Although, even I would have to contest the fact I have a tender soul.*

Gwyneth gives a wistful shake of the head. *There's been a man or two I would have gladly helped to the other side. Of course, I would never be silly enough to get caught. Murder is the kind of thing you need to give serious thought to. I'd make arrangements to have someone else take the fall. It would be an expert move. No room for a sophomoric blunder. All things would have to be considered from every angle. The target would need to have lots of enemies. The poor soul I'd pin the crime on would have to be an easy target themselves. Perhaps lots of angry ex-wives.* She raises a glass to my father before taking a quick sip of her drink.

Dear Lord, my father is in mortal danger around this woman.

Although, she does bring up a good point. If you were going to pin a murder on someone, they'd have to be an easy target.

Nessa was an easy target. Nessa was angry with Shelby. That wasn't a secret. Everyone knew she worked at the inn. And if she were there, her gun would be, too.

Camila shakes her head at me. "What makes you think Jasper arrested the wrong person?"

My mouth falls open as I look to Jasper. "That's not what I said."

Camila tips her head my way. "But that's what you meant, isn't it?"

"Yes, but—"

Camila leans in, her eyes locked over Jasper's. "Not once did I question your acumen for doing your job. Bizzy, are you suggesting he's less than capable?"

"No." It comes out crisp and a touch too loud. "I'm suggesting that people, science even, can make mistakes. They can be deceived. I think whoever killed Shelby used Nessa because they thought she was an easy target."

Gwyneth straightens. "That's what I would have done," she declares with a touch of surprise.

Dad leans my way. "Bizzy, do you feel safe at the inn? That's two homicides back to back right here in Cider Cove—at your inn."

"I'm fine," I say. I'm about to extrapolate on the fact when Gwyneth looks to Camila with a touch of horror.

"My goodness, Camila, do you feel safe at the inn? It never occurred to me not to feel safe there."

Camila chortles a dark laugh. "I have a concealed carry permit. I have my special little friend with me wherever I go. I feel more than safe."

Camila has a gun? And she wasn't sorry that Shelby was dead? Maybe I should revisit these pictures Shelby suggested she take. *Huh.*

Jasper offers me a hint of a smile just as dinner arrives.

Perfect, he muses. *We can eat and get out of this mess. I'll talk football or golf, or the moon landing with her father until it's time to hit the door. I just hope Bizzy speaks to me after this disaster.*

I nod over to him, reassuring him I would.

And Jasper does just that. He and Dad talk about everything under the sun—or should I say moon, while Camila and Gwyneth exchange odd catty little barbs that are almost worth the price of admission.

Who knew a twist of events would lead a man to wedge himself between these two scheming vixens? And to think that man is my father. Actually, that doesn't surprise me all that much. He's been known to cause a kerfuffle or two amongst the fairer sex.

Dinner wraps up and my father and Jasper each drop a wad of bills onto the table—and honestly, none of us can get out of here quick enough.

We pass Leo and Mack on the way out, both of whom are staring deeply into one another's eyes.

I think Leo is getting lucky tonight.

Here's hoping, he says. *By the way, your meal looked exhausting. I hope you get some rest, Bizzy.*

Thank you. My night can only go up from here.

And it does. Gwyneth and Dad go for a stroll down Main Street while Camila stalks off in a huff.

And soon enough, it's just Jasper and me.

I wrap my arms around this tall, strong, and far too handsome man by my side.

"For the record, Detective, I don't believe for a minute that you're less than capable."

His lids hood low as a wicked smile crests his lips.

"How about we go back to my place and I show you just how capable I am?"

"And how would that be?" My eyes widen as I tremble out a short-lived laugh.

"Maybe I should demonstrate." He lands a kiss to my lips.

"Okay. I'm in." I run my finger down his tie. "I'm sure you'll show me how capable the rest of you is soon enough."

He gives a crooked grin. "You just gave me something to look forward to."

"Me, too."

We head back to his place—mostly because it's lacking three pairs of roving eyes and Jasper makes good on his word.

And he is very, very capable with his mouth.

With his career? I'm not so sure.

The only thing Nessa Crosby is guilty of is being an easy target.

And I'm about to prove it.

CHAPTER 13

*I*t took less than sixty seconds of convincing to have Leo Granger join me in heading over to the Harris Financial office building.

I wasn't kidding when I told him that I would be looking for his help. And thankfully, he's not hesitating in giving it to me.

Leo gives an unwarranted grin out at the tall building paneled in mirrors. He's ditched his deputy wear for a monkey suit and looks surprisingly dapper. I'm sure he'll garner more than a few glances from the women inside.

"I scoured all of Shelby Harris' social media sites and didn't see a single picture of Luke anywhere," I say. "Don't you think that's weird?"

"No." Leo looks bored by the idea in general. "I went over her stuff, too. She liked pretty things. Luke is a dude. Dudes aren't pretty."

"Maybe. Maybe not. From what I could tell, most of these influencers had a handful of pictures snuggling with their boyfriends. I just find it odd that he was nowhere to be seen. Something doesn't sit right about this. Shelby had her entire life on display. Why not her shiny new boyfriend?"

"Let's ask the shiny new boyfriend." Leo goes to open his door and I land my hand over his arm to stop him.

"Not so fast, Deputy Granger. Now that I have you alone in the privacy of your truck, I want you to tell me about the other transmundane classifications." I still can't wrap my head around the fact I'm something called telesensual. It sounds dark and mysterious, two words I'd hardly use to describe myself.

Leo relaxes back in his seat. "Okay, keep in mind I gleaned all this from my aunt—she's dying to meet you, by the way. She and Georgie are fast friends."

"Lovely. I can't see a single thing that can go wrong with this."

He chuckles at the thought. "Okay, there are the visionaries— people who can see things that are about to happen, have happened, or are happening somewhere outside of their current location. I don't know much about them. Then there are the sibylline—those who have a knowing about things that are about to transpire. And the most interesting in my book—the supersensuals. People who can communicate with the dead."

"The dead?" I all but shout the words. Good call on having this little talk in the safety of his pickup.

"I agree with you there." He gives a little wink, acknowledging the fact he just read my mind. "Don't worry. It's not a catching condition. I've done some research and no one has two gifts, let alone all. We've got what we've got."

"I won't complain. Although, it's not always a gift, is it?"

He offers a morose smile. "No, Bizzy. It's not."

I sigh as I look out at the building before us. "Let's head on in."

He pauses a moment as if he were rethinking the entire plan. "What would Jasper say if he knew what we were doing?"

"Not much, because he's never going to find out. I've sworn you to secrecy, remember?"

That smarmy grin he's been wearing like a Halloween mask glides off his face. "I'd like to advise against that."

A laugh gets caught in my throat. "I bet you would. In fact, I bet that's the real reason you agreed to come out with me. You just can't wait to stir the pot between Jasper and me. What is it with you two anyway that you just can't stand to see him happy?"

His head inches back a notch. "That's not true. I'll be the first to admit what happened between Camila and me was a big mistake. I wasn't thinking straight. She assured me they were over. I should have cleared things with Jasper. Instead, I took a risk and it didn't pay off. I lost my best friend over nothing. Jasper and I were closer than brothers."

"That's funny, he said the very same thing about you. And you should know—you were there prying into his mind just like I was."

His chest rises and falls with his next breath. "Well, it's true. And believe me, I'm going to fix this mess. It will take time, but if we can get even halfway to where we once were, I'll take it. There's nothing worse than being frozen out in no man's land. Which brings me to the point I was making. If you don't tell Jasper what you were doing with me, you're taking the same risk I was."

The thought sends a chill through me. In no way do I want to end up in the outs with Jasper.

"Fine. I'll tell him. As soon as the real killer is apprehended. Someone is setting Nessa up, but he's too stubborn to hear it. And that's exactly why I have you here. We'll go up like we talked about and ask to speak with Luke about a loan for a boat."

"A boat. Right." He gives a tug at his lapels. "After you, Mrs. Granger."

"No, no." I swat him on the arm. "I can't be Mrs. Granger. Jasper will come after you with a hatchet for making me pretend to be your missus. We're just—dating or something."

Leo shakes his head as we head into the warm building and step onto the polished elevator.

"Fine"—he says—"we're just dating or something."

"Hey, Leo? Did you know Camila has a concealed carry permit? She has a gun with her at all times."

"Yup." He nonchalantly nods at a woman walking past us.

"Did you know she knew Shelby Harris? And that she wasn't all that sorry she was dead? She mentioned something about Shelby connecting her to a photographer. Do you think that's somehow connected to why she didn't care for Shelby?"

He stops in his tracks, his eyes staring off into some unknown horizon. "I never heard anything about this. But Camila isn't a killer."

"How do you know?" I pull out my phone. "How can I find the photographer? Or even the pictures she took? I bet Chelsea Ashley might know. Or maybe I should just google Camila's name." I do just that and Leo scoffs.

"You're not going to find the photographer that way."

"You're right. It's just a bunch of links to her social media profiles and school functions through the Sheffield School Dist —" I don't even finish my sentence before I hit pay dirt. "Oh my, wow." A laugh bubbles from me as I follow the link at the bottom. "Ms. February *Gear Head* calendar, the naughty school mistress, Camila Ryder."

"What?" Leo leans in as I hold the phone up where he can see it for himself. There she is in full color, leaning over a desk with a pencil in her hair. She's donned a short plaid skirt and has her white button-down blouse cinched in a knot just above her belly button.

Leo moans and shakes his head. "I'm not touching this one. You're on your own if you want to bring this up to her. This is recent. I bet Jasper doesn't know about it either. Just remember, she has a gun." A playful smile blinks on his lips. "But she didn't kill Shelby. My guess is she's hoping this goes unnoticed and eventually goes away. This is something she could lose her job over. I don't know what she was thinking." The elevator opens up and we step inside. "Let's focus on this right now."

"Fine. I'll take care of Camila later." On my own.

The elevator vomits us out into a spacious, bright environment with a white enameled reception desk ready to greet us. A garland of silk fall leaves lines the counter, along with a witch sitting on a pumpkin and a couple of mesh ghosts that look as if they're about to topple over.

A brunette with a bright blue jacket and matching framed glasses sits up at attention. There's a gold nameplate on her chest that reads CAROL in all capital letters. And as soon as we let her know we're here to see Luke about a loan, she rolls her eyes.

I lean in. "Not a lot of faith in the guy, I take it?"

She gives a quick glance over her shoulder. "It's not that. It's just he's sort of a scumbag." She mouths those last few words out. "But you're in the right place. He's a genius at directing people where to go. He hasn't been in the loan biz all that long, so I guess you can say he doesn't quite have the hang of it." She squints over at Leo for a moment. "Come to think of it, you're the first people who have ever asked to speak with him in person."

She stands and motions for us to follow along. "Usually I call ahead to see if they're busy, but with this bozo, I think we'll just surprise him in his natural habitat—video games."

We hit the end of the hall and she swings the door open wide. "Got a client!" she honks out and he freezes.

There he is with his blond hair rumpled, socks sitting on top of his desk, a game controller in his hand, and his laptop opened, blaring music as if it were a heavy metal concert.

"Geez." He quickly steps into his shoes and slams the laptop shut just as Carol entombs us inside the room with him. "Hey." He motions for us to take a seat. "What can I do for you?" He extends a hand to each of us and we're quick to shake it.

There's something boyish about Luke in general with his wavy, sun-kissed hair, his round, clean-shaven face.

Leo presses out a wide grin. "My girlfriend is finally letting me get a boat."

"Finally?" I lean back, not amused with the unfavorable light he's chosen to paint me in.

Leo shoots me a look. "Don't start getting on my back again." He shakes his head over at Luke. "Women, right?"

Luke barks out a laugh. "I feel ya. In fact, I think we're going to get along just fine."

I tap my knee to Leo's. *Why did you have to go in that direction?*

What? His lips twitch with a sly smile. *You said you didn't want to be the missus. Besides, most girlfriends are not big proponents of being replaced with a large water vessel.*

I avert my eyes at that one.

Luke examines us both. "A boat is a beautiful thing. In fact, it's the next toy on my list."

Leo nods. "So your wife won't mind."

"You know what they say—what she doesn't know won't hurt her." He pulls out a couple of forms from the filing cabinet.

Hey—I'm back to tapping Leo's knee with mine—*he doesn't have a wife. He had a girlfriend.*

Leo shrugs. *I don't think he's too interested in getting into the details of his grisly love life. I get it. The guy is grieving. He's probably not thinking straight.*

"Here you go." Luke sets a stack of applications in front of Leo. *All right, time to get the message across. We're done here.* He offers an affable grin our way.

There's an all-around frat boy vibe about him. I don't like to say it, but he sort of has a face people love to hate. The perpetual bad boy. And it makes me wonder exactly how bad he can be.

Leo lifts a brow my way. *This is your moment, kid. Do or die.*

I bite down over my lower lip when Leo calls me *kid*. He can't be more than a few years older than me. It seems silly and adorable all at the same time.

"You know"—I tip my head over at Luke—"there's something very familiar about you."

Luke's suit jacket splits as his chest expands with pride. "I get that all the time. Everyone I meet wonders if they went to high school with me. I must have that kind of face." He slaps his cheek playfully.

"No, that's not it." I pause just long enough to look as if I'm trying to place him. "Oh, I remember. You were at that women's conference at the Country Cottage Inn—the one featuring Ginger King on how to land a rich man."

Luke tips his head back a notch, his face quickly bleaching out. "Right. I wasn't there trying to pick up on any pointers, though."

The three of us share a warm laugh.

Luke sniffs hard. "I was actually there with my girlfriend." His affect dims quickly. "She was—um"—he slaps the back of his neck—"Shelby was the one that was killed that night."

My hand clutches at my chest. "I'm so very sorry." I lean. "You know, I was a follower of hers—on her social media sites. I've seen almost all of her pictures. I don't remember seeing you."

His chest pumps with the idea of a laugh. "No, you won't find any. I didn't want to be a part of her overexposed world."

"Don't blame you. And I'm sorry for your loss as well." Leo nods as he offers his sympathy. "What happened? I mean, that was a terrible thing. Was it a robbery gone wrong? Was she assaulted?"

"No." His brows dip down in the middle as he grows visibly upset. "It wasn't anything like that. I don't know what happened. I was trying to get her alone, and no matter how hard I tried, she kept evading me. Eventually, I followed her out of the ballroom and she bolted out of sight."

I glance to Leo. *He told Jasper he saw Nessa arguing with Shelby in the courtyard.*

Leo shakes his head. *Maybe that's as far as he wants to take the conversation with us. Give him something to think about.*

"I can't imagine what you must be going through," I say,

studying his face as if I were trying to determine whether a word coming out of his mouth were the truth. "It must be agonizing for you."

He shakes his head. *You don't know the half of it, lady.*

"Were you the one who found her body?" I can feel my own body growing hot, because I'm not entirely sure Luke doesn't realize that *I'm* the one that found the body.

"No. I don't know who did. The entire thing was a nightmare from the moment I heard the gunshot."

"You heard the gunshot?"

"It was powerful. I wasn't sure what direction it came from, so initially I went the other way. But it only took a few minutes for me to find her. There was already a crowd around her at that point."

"So, you were never in the courtyard?" It comes out incredulous, partly because I can't wrap my head around this. He's either lying to Jasper or me.

Leo takes a breath. *My guess is you. He owes you nothing.*

"Nope." Luke leans back in his seat. *I'm not admitting anything. It's bad enough I told the cops what I did. Nessa—arrested for murder one. I'm not sure if it's a blessing or a curse at this point. For all I know, she didn't say anything about Sarah to anyone. From now on, I know nothing about nothing. I can't lose this job. I can't rock the boat any more than I have. One more unsteady step and I'll be overboard and eaten by sharks.*

Leo lands a hand on the table and pats it. "I just hope the last memory you had together was a good one." He hitches his head my way. "All this one and I do is bicker. With our luck, we'd have a major blowout right before something tragic like that happened."

Luke flinches as if Leo had struck him. "You guessed it. And it wasn't pretty. But I'm keeping my mouth shut about it. Her dad runs this place. The last thing he needs to know is that she was at her wits' end with me." *That it was over. Sarah contacted her in the middle of that stupid seminar and Shelby flipped her lid—of course, nosey Nessa heard us arguing about her. Shelby was about to blow my cover sky-high. Honestly, if she weren't dead, I would be. It couldn't have been pretty. I guess in that sense, one of us had to go.*

Leo and I exchange a brief glance.

My phone buzzes in my hand and it's a text from Jasper. **Stopped by the inn to say hello. Emmie mentioned you went to Seaview with some guy. Granger is missing. Please tell me he hasn't hijacked you this afternoon.**

Every last part of me freezes in horror.

Just a second. I text back and slip the phone into my purse because I don't have it in me to lie to Jasper.

Leo leans his elbow onto Luke's desk. "You knew your girlfriend pretty well. Did she have any enemies? Anybody at all who would want to hurt her? If there wasn't a robbery and she wasn't assaulted, it must have been personal."

Luke glances out the window. "Oh, it was personal. I know that for a fact. I wasn't the only one in a heated argument with her that night. In fact, I saw the woman who was speaking that night have it out with her. A couple of others, too."

"Ginger King?" I ask, surprised to hear her name mentioned in an unfavorable light—not that there's much favorable about her.

"Yup. That's the one. The rich hubby chaser. Shelby said they used to be close—real close. In fact, Ginger was using Shelby's new dog at her seminars to make herself more likable. Trust me. There's not a dog on the planet who can achieve that feat."

I'd have to agree with him there.

A part of me is afraid he'll ask to have Peanut. Not that I'd ever comply. I don't have a good feeling about this guy in general. Besides, he's a big fake, sitting in here all day playing video games, collecting a paycheck for essentially dating the boss' daughter. And I suppose that's all about to crash to an end for him.

Leo shakes his head. "What would Ginger and your girlfriend have to argue about?"

"The dog?" I offer and immediately regret it.

Leo thumps my knee with his. *Never give the suspect a way out.*

Luke looks to the ceiling. *I should just go with it and say the dog.* "Not the dog." He grimaces as if he were in pain. "There was something going on between the two of them. Shelby never wanted to talk about it, but whatever it was, it steamed her. She said something a few days before she died that the truth was about to come out and Ginger wouldn't like it." He pinches his eyes shut a moment. "I'm sorry. It's all upsetting me. I don't want to talk about it anymore." *I need to think about my next move. The only truth I care about is the truth she had on me. Had that gotten out, it would be my funeral next week. Not hers.*

Luke walks us to the door, and Leo and I head for the safety of the elevator.

"Well, Detective Baker?" He presses out a short-lived grin. "What's the verdict?"

"He has a secret, so he could be guilty. He could have done it. I'll make notes once I get home and cross-check everything I've learned so far." I pull out my phone. "But first, I gotta deal with a little guilt myself." I flash Jasper's text at Leo and he cringes.

"Squash that bug, Bizzy. Before your relationship ends up getting squashed instead."

Leo and I drive back to Cider Cove in silence.

And the both of us feel as if we're about to see the heel of Jasper's shoe.

CHAPTER 14

"*P*rotection?" Jasper is unfairly handsome while conducting his interrogation of me. Okay, fine. He's not exactly patting me down—not that I would object to the endeavor.

"Yes. Protection," I say, cinching my arms around him.

Fish huffs and it sounds like a sneeze. *You don't need protection, Bizzy*, she yowls it out so Sherlock and Peanut can hear. *You're a strong girl. You can take care of yourself.*

Peanut whimpers as he walks in a small circle before burying his face in his tail. *My poor Shelby needed protection. I couldn't bear it if anything happened to you.*

Sherlock takes a seat next to Peanut. *All Bizzy needs is Jasper.* It comes out just shy of a howl.

Fish hops over and yowls again. *You mean, all Jasper needs is Bizzy.*

As soon as I got back, I asked Jasper to meet me at my cottage and he met me at the door before I could get the key into the lock. And now we're standing smack in the middle of it with our arms wrapped around one another while I try to dance my way out of a Leo Granger pothole I inadvertently fell in.

His lips purse to the side, and something about the action makes my insides bisect with heat.

It's not fair that Jasper Wilder has the power to bring me to my knees with just a simple facial gesture.

"Bizzy." Jasper closes his eyes as a sigh depresses from him. "You know I can't with a clear conscience encourage you to go after a suspect."

"Believe me, I don't need your encouragement." I feel terrible just saying it. "How about you build a fire and I'll get us some hot cider? Meet you on the sofa in a minute."

And we do just that. Jasper has the fire crackling with life as we settle in close with a cup of steaming cider in each of our hands. Georgie gave me half a dozen of her flannel, toilet paper pumpkins and I lined them in a row across the coffee table.

I happened to have a plateful of Emmie's pumpkin spice mini muffins in the kitchen, and so I hand-feed one to Jasper and he does the same for me. I bite down gently on his finger and hold him hostage for a moment.

A crooked smile glides up the side of his face.

"So, what did you glean?" Jasper watches me as he takes a careful sip from his mug. *What I really wanted to ask was why Leo? What's going on with him? Between the two of them? I blame Leo for whatever it is.*

Here we go. "First, I want to talk about Leo." Leo was right. I need to squash this bug before it squashes all the good things I'm fighting to have with Jasper. "I thought since I was headed out to Luke's office, I needed a good cover. We told him we were shopping for a boat. We needed a loan."

We. His lids lower a notch, and I can feel his rage against Leo percolating.

"And I'm sorry. I probably should have brought Georgie with me, or Macy or Emmie. But Macy and Emmie were swamped, and all Leo does is hang around the inn. He said the department stationed him here."

145

Jasper gives a slow blink. "And that would be because I requested it." *Of all the deputies to send. Come to think of it, I bet Leo volunteered.* He shakes his head as if just coming to this conclusion. "I'll be honest. I'm glad he was with you."

"What?" My heart gives an unnatural thump, half-afraid he's going to dump me and head straight to Camila's room.

"Yes." He sets down his cider and I do the same. "Leo may have been in plain clothes, but he was armed. I'd hate to think if you went out with Georgie and things went south. But"—he lands his lips to mine—"the last thing I want is you teaming up with Leo and the two of you running around interrogating suspects together."

"It won't happen again." I'm quick to shake my head.

"I know it won't." Jasper's tone is serious to the bone. "I'll have him removed from the force if he pulls that stunt again."

I suck in a quick breath. "Jasper. That's terrible." My mind reels at the thought of putting Leo's career in jeopardy. "Please don't threaten him. I'll leave him be. I won't ask him for any more favors."

I'm glad about it. But I'm not saying a word. A thought comes to me. "You're going back to utilizing Macy and Emmie, aren't you?"

"You forgot Georgie."

"*Bizzy.*" He's right back to closing his eyes. "Okay. Fine. That just means I need to solve the case quicker. Let's crack this nut." He wraps his arms around me. "What happened with Luke today?"

"The guy is a character." I quickly fill him in on the fact Luke implied that Ginger and Shelby had something they were hiding. "He said he really didn't want to admit to anything—that it was bad enough that he told the cops what he did. He said he felt terrible for Nessa. Oh, and he also said that if Shelby wasn't dead, he would be. He made it sound as if whatever Shelby was furious with him about that night was enough to end him."

Jasper blinks as if he were surprised. "You got him to say all that? You're pretty good at getting people to open up."

As much as I want to smile, my lips knot up instead. The truth is, Luke didn't share half of that with me. I took it right from his mind.

"Ginger and Shelby had a secret." Jasper jots it down into his phone. "Luke has a secret, and he's glad Shelby isn't around to tell it." He looks my way. "Is there anything else you can remember? Anything at all?"

I think on it a moment.

"Yes, actually." I lift a finger with the memory. "He mentioned someone named Sarah. He said Sarah contacted Shelby in the middle of Ginger's seminar, and that's what made Shelby flip out."

Jasper's eyes widen a notch. "Boy, you really cast a spell." He picks up another mini muffin. "You didn't feed him one of these, did you? Are you lacing them with truth serum?"

"Very funny."

"I'm serious. It's as if you strolled into Luke Parker's office and read his mind or something."

My stomach rolls at the thought of being exposed. Although, in truth, I'd love nothing more than to fill Jasper in on my secret. It's always felt heavy keeping my lips sealed. But now with Leo in the know, it suddenly feels as if I've got a battleship on my shoulders.

Fish, Sherlock, and Peanut all scuttle forward and sit in a line as they watch with bated breath.

Fish lets out a fierce meow. *Are you going to do it, Bizzy? Are you going to tell him he's right?*

Sherlock lets out a little bark. *This is exciting. Jasper will know! Jasper will know!*

Peanut whines, *What will happen when he finds out? What will happen to you, Bizzy? What will happen to us?*

Peanut has me giving some serious pause—or should I say *paws* to the situation.

"What do we do with this information, Jasper? How do you make heads or tails out of the pieces?"

He furrows his brows. "Do you have your laptop handy?"

"I sure do." I pluck it from the sofa table and open it up. "Now what?"

"Let's do a quick search on Luke Parker."

I type in his name and nothing.

"Wow," I say. "I've never seen anyone with such a small cyber footprint."

"*Huh.*" Jasper leans in. "Okay, so we'll mark him off as a dead end for now. Type in *Shelby Harris.*"

"That will be a contrast. She was basically the queen of the internet." I look her up, and sure enough she's everywhere.

"Head over a few pages. I find the deeper I dig, the more interesting things get."

The first few pages are all links that lead back to her social media sites. That is, until we stumble upon something out of the ordinary.

"Jasper, look at this," I say, clicking the link that says *Whaler's Cove Community College.* "It lists Shelby Harris as an English TA about five years ago."

Jasper leans in. "Now there's something new." He jots it down into his phone.

"Do you think it's important?"

"One thing I have learned after doing this for nearly a decade is that you never know what little detail can turn the whole case on its ear."

"Then I'll tuck it in the back of my mind." We do a quick search on Ginger and yield nothing. "Do you see the irony here between Luke and Ginger? Luke has zero info out there compared to Ginger who has at least fifty pages, and yet we yield just about as much on her as we did on Luke. It's just a bunch of selfies and info on that gold digger's guide she's pushing. I can't believe she's making a killing off telling girls how to marry a rich man."

"Evidently, it's information some women are willing to pay for. At the end of the day, Ginger King is a businesswoman."

"Yeah, and a darn good one." Chelsea comes to mind. "I'll look up Chelsea Ashley." I input her name, and both Jasper and I hold our breath at what the first page exposes. "Jasper, is this a real mug shot?"

"Sure as heck looks like it. What was she arrested for?"

I click into the article. "Top millennial influencer busted for shoplifting fine jewelry." My mouth falls open. "Do you think this is the dark secret she was keeping for Shelby?" Another thought comes to me. "Ginger mentioned that Shelby stole from the open houses Scout was conducting. But when they got busted, it was Scout who took the rap. Shelby was vindictive in making sure she kept her secret. I bet she did the same thing to Chelsea. Would that be a big enough motive for murder?"

"Sure. Revenge. Damaging a reputation. It all fits. But with so many different motives, we need to somehow winnow it down to who really did it. I'll tell you right now, it makes things tough when there was so much strife between Shelby and her friends."

The name Luke was thinking about comes back to me. "What about that Sarah woman Luke mentioned? How do we find anything on her?"

"That's a tough one. Maybe type their names in together."

"Sarah and Luke Parker," I say as I input their names and a group of images pop up just above a scant number of links. "Jasper, that's Luke." My adrenaline spikes as I click into the picture, and just like that my mouth falls open. "Oh my goodness, Jasper. This is why Luke Parker has no cyber footprint."

He takes a deep breath. "And now we know exactly who Sarah is."

CHAPTER 15

*L*uke Parker isn't Luke Parker at all. He's Luke Abernathy —a very much in debt, very much married, father to four-year-old twin boys. No wonder he didn't want his picture anywhere near Shelby's social media. It would have been a dead giveaway.

"Wow." Georgie shudders as I run all this by her. "You and Detective Hot Stuff felt all this out last night?" Her left brow hooks into her forehead. "What else did you happen to feel out?" She elbows me in the ribs as she tries her best to find out if we moved the needle on our relationship.

"Don't get too excited, Georgie. We're still firmly planted on first base."

Georgie makes a face just as a small crowd moves over toward the register in the Country Cottage Café and we step aside so that they can put in their orders. Emmie is at the helm and the entire café holds the hypnotic scent of fresh pumpkin spice mini muffins.

Georgie grunts, "Okay, so first base isn't a bad place to be. But get *busy*, would you, Bizzy?" She howls with laughter. "See what I did there?" She steps in close. "What do we do now?"

Fish wraps herself around my ankles and I pick her up. "Right now, I want to track down his wife, Sarah Abernathy, and grill her a bit. You know, get into Luke's psyche from another angle."

Fish licks her lips as she looks up at me. *Good thinking, Bizzy. I've met my fair share of fat cats who like to run around. And he sounds like one of them.*

I nod down at her. Fish has always been wise beyond her years—or months, considering she's just a kitten.

"I wasn't talking about the killer." Georgie scoffs as she tucks her fists into her hips. "What do we do about you and Detective Kisses-a-Lot? Macy's already scored three home runs in the past week alone. You're down three, and next up at bat, Biz. I say we spruce up your nighttime accouterments and slam one out of the park."

I make a face as I look past her at the crowd. "Never mind about Jasper and me. He still needs to call off his ex. And maybe his mother. Until then, we're still not officially official, so the people in the grandstands can put away their mitts. I'm not knocking anything out of the park anytime soon." And every cell in my body is protesting the idea.

"You're no fun," she grunts as she pulls out her phone. "I'll do a little digging and find out where to find this Sarah chick." She strays off to an empty table just as Emmie's brother, Jordy, heads this way. Both his flannel and jeans look as if he was rolling around in the grass. His face looks as if it has just enough grime on it to make his blue eyes glow like lanterns.

"Hey, Bizzy. I just cut back the hedges, mowed the lawn, and fixed the fountain out front. The Montgomerys sent another truck full of pumpkins. They said they had a surplus and thought you could use them. Where do you want them?"

Fish smacks me with her tail. *Put them in front of our cottage. I do like to hide and give the dogs a decent fright every now and again. I need the cover.*

"Another truck full? We've already blanketed the front and the back of the inn. Not to mention I've dotted them everywhere I can inside. Aside from putting a few big ones in front of my cottage"—I land a kiss to Fish's furry head—"what do you think we should do with them?"

Jordy thinks about it. "You're having that party in a couple of days, right?"

"The mixer. I almost forgot all about it. Ginger King invited all her fans, and Carter O' Riley is coming in strong with his testosterone brigade. It's a costume party. I have a feeling things are going to get wild. I just hope the ballroom can contain them all."

This is going to be fun, Bizzy. Good luck trying to lock me up in the cottage for that one. I'll be front and center. I'll keep an eye out for a madman with a gun in the event they come back to claim another victim. You never know. It could be you.

I wrinkle my nose at Fish before setting her down.

Jordy shakes his head. "The ballroom might get stuffy by the end of the night. How about we open the back doors and have the party flood out into the courtyard? We can use the pumpkins to decorate it. I'll fill the planter beds and as many empty baskets as I can. I'll call some friends and we'll carve the rest and have them lit that night. If you let me get really creative, I'll turn the forest that butts up to the courtyard into a haunted woods for the night. I've got a fog machine and purple twinkle lights. It'll look like magic. Black magic."

"Sounds terrifyingly perfect. Do it," I say.

Jordy takes off and I spot Camila just finishing up a conversation on her phone before hanging up and walking this way.

"Camila." I try my best to sound perky. "Can I speak with you a minute?"

She shakes out her long dark hair as if trying to ward off a gnat. Why do I get the feeling I'm a gnat?

"What?" she snaps in annoyance.

"It's just, I, uh—my brother, Huxley, subscribes to *Gear Head* magazine, and he's such a good customer they've already sent him a calendar for next year."

She sucks in a quick breath and drags me off into the quiet hush of the hallway.

"You know, don't you?" Her eyes sparkle like shards of glass, and if I didn't know better, I'd say they were tears. *I wish I never met Shelby Harris. If she wasn't already dead, I'd—I'd...* She sags as if she couldn't possibly finish the thought.

"I know." I give a guilty shrug. "But I won't say anything to Jasper."

"You bet you won't." The words come out like a threat, and somehow I think she means it just that way. "Look, I made a huge mistake. It could cost me everything. I'll lose my position at the school. I'll have nowhere to turn."

"You have my word. Your secret is safe with me." As safe as it can be until February. "Camila, can I ask why you would do something like this? I mean, you said yourself it could cost you your career."

She closes her eyes a moment. "Would you believe me if I said I had no idea the picture would be published?"

"Did you sign a release? Are they using your image illegally? My brother, Huxley, is a lawyer. I'm sure he can—"

"Yes, I signed a release," she snips. "And I don't care very much for your brother, Huxley, at the moment. He can shove his legal degree. Those pictures were taken after a very long day of shooting very demure pictures for a women's catalog. At the end of the day, the photographer asked if I wanted to have a little fun and I said yes. The release was for all images. I didn't realize that at the time. And ironically, none of the demure pictures made it into any catalog."

"Camila, you were taken advantage of."

She glares at me a moment. "Thank you for pointing that out. And now, I would like to forget it. In the meantime, I'll be running scared for the rest of my time as a high school guidance counselor because obviously my days are numbered."

"And Shelby Harris was the one to connect you with the photographer." I nod as all the pieces come in crystal clear.

"Don't get any funny ideas, busy bee. I didn't kill anybody. And if you so much as whisper the idea to anyone, I'll make sure that on the day I lose my job—you lose yours." *You'll lose Jasper regardless.* "Whoever killed Shelby is still out there." *And if she cost them as much as she cost me, I just might be rooting for them to get away with murder.*

She stalks past me and heads back upstairs in a flurry.

Camila sounds innocent. But that doesn't mean I'm so willing to wipe her off my suspect list.

As much as I'd like to gnaw on everything that just happened, I spot my not-so-sweet floozy of a sister talking to Emmie, so I head on over.

"Heard you hit a triple header," I say before making a face at this older, questionably wiser blonde-haired version of me. "Wait, that's not right. I meant, I heard you hit three homers."

Macy tugs a lock of her short hair. "You had it right the first time. But I'm done with him now." She flicks her wrist as if it were a passing faze.

"What? You can't be done with him. That's Jasper's brother. You can't use him and lose him. It's going to make Thanksgiving dinner really, really awkward."

Macy blinks back. "Relax. We were having a good time. It's not like we have twelve kids and I'm kicking him to the curb."

Emmie leans in. "He's the lawyer, right? Kick him my way. I saw him at the Haunted Harvest Festival. I wouldn't mind sinking my fangs into him."

"That's because he looks exactly like Jasper," I'm quick to point out. "And we've always liked the same thing."

"You want him?" Macy tips her head to Emmie and coos as if she were giving a puppy away to a good home. "He's all yours.

Just remember, don't feed him after midnight. Unless, of course, you don't have an early schedule."

Emmie claps like a seal. "Hear that, Bizzy? I've got me a Wilder."

My eyes widen a notch. "Emmie, you don't want Macy's sloppy seconds. And Macy, what if he's still into you? You're going to break his heart." I'd like to break her neck, but I leave that fun little homicidal fact out of it for now. "A part of me wishes you never threw your unmentionables at Jasper's brother."

Macy rolls her eyes. "Calm down, panty patrol. Besides, Emmie deserves to have a little fun." She turns to Emmie. "And Jamison is all about making sure you have a very good time."

Emmie squeals at the racy revelation. "Invite him to the party this Saturday night. The inn is hosting its first Halloween rager."

A fountain of words tries to bubble up my throat all at once. "I seriously doubt this will be a rager. And it's not our party to invite people to."

Look who's here, Bizzy! Fish says from somewhere below. *She tried on the witch's hat in front and it fit! Peanut says she's the real deal. He said I should watch my furry back before she makes me her familiar.*

A sugary breeze catches my attention as Ginger King with all her fiery redheaded glory pops up next to me.

"Are you talking about my party?" Ginger spikes a black glossy fingernail into her chest. "Please, invite whomever you want."

Fish claws at my boot and I quickly pick her up.

"Thank you, Ginger," I say. "That's kind of you to offer."

"I mean it." She makes a sour face at Fish. "I'm having the café cater the event. Just add whatever you think we'll need. Carter is bringing the boys. So I don't expect any one of you to be single by the end of the night." She gives a sly wink to Emmie and Macy, both of whom gurgle with titillation at the prospect.

Wonderful.

Macy plucks out her phone. "I'll invite all the Wilders since we're pretty close now. Plus, that way I can try out Dalton. A man who specializes in touchdowns should never be underestimated." She takes off toward Georgie. "I'll invite Mom, too!"

Good Lord. Jasper will never speak to me again after Macy runs his brothers over with her unstoppable libido.

Emmie leans in. "How about you, Ginger? How's your love life? I bet you've got a line of rich men a mile long all waiting to make you their own."

"I've got my sights set on someone in particular, and I'm about to head over to the Seaview Sherriff's Department to extend a personal invite to the party."

Emmie gasps, "Is it that hot deputy that's been hanging around? Leo Granger?"

Ginger looks as if she's been offended. "What's a Granger? Anyway, no. It's Detective Wilder."

Emmie and I exchange a quick glance, and Fish yowls right at Ginger for even thinking of conducting the malfeasance.

Don't let her near him, Bizzy. She's bound to cast a spell on him.

Ginger purrs, "He's got that naughty haughty gleam in his eyes every time he looks at me, and I just melt right into a puddle."

I know exactly what she's talking about because he happens to melt me the same way. But what Ginger doesn't realize is that Jasper is simply being himself. He can't help it if he's arrestingly handsome. Ironic, since he does walk around with a set of shiny bracelets to do just that—arrest.

"Anyway"—she points to Emmie—"two dozen of those pumpkin *spell* mini muffins, please."

Spell? Fish perks an ear up. *I knew it. She's trying to cast a pox over your man. Don't give her anything delicious to take with her.*

Emmie shrugs over at me. "Two dozen mini muffins coming right up." She takes off.

"I spoke to Nessa this morning." I offer a forlorn smile.

"You did?" Ginger looks aghast as if I just told her I went to the morgue and spoke to Shelby herself.

I nod. "She sounded absolutely miserable. She's convinced she's going to spend the rest of her life behind bars."

Ginger scoffs. "As she should. People can't just get away with murder these days."

Especially not Nessa. Nope. That little beanpole is going to fry for this one.

I feel terrible that she thinks Nessa did this. That just about *everyone* thinks Nessa did this. I seem to be the only one that's not convinced. But I decide to drop it for now.

"Back to the party," I start. "Since you've kindly opened the doors, how about you write up a cute little invite that I can share with the guests of the inn? I know a lot of them are your fans and they'd appreciate having you personally invite them to the party. Maybe you could start it off with *it will be a dark and stormy night.* Or *once upon a cursed night in Cider Cove*, or—"

She waves me off. "Please. I couldn't write my way out of a paper bag. Just send a mass text with the time and place. That's all I've done so far, and all of my fans will be there. We can call it something cute like the Monster Mash. Can't wait until Detective Wilder sees me in my barely-there bunny costume. I have a feeling my night is going to be a real *scream*, if you know what I mean."

Emmie pops up with a box of those mini muffins, and Ginger is quick to pay her.

She leans my way. "Wish me luck." She takes off before I can say another word.

Fish swipes the air in her direction. *Let me go, Bizzy. I'll have Sherlock bite her ankles on the way out.*

"How very catty," I say. "I think I like this side of you," I whisper to my sweet kitten just as she jumps out of my arms and scampers for the reception area.

Georgie crops up, wagging my phone. "I found her, Bizzy. I found her!"

"Found who?"

"The girl with the twins. She's a part of some moms group. Mama Bears of Edison. I joined the group and they just let me in. They're having a play date at the Haunted Harvest Festival today. They've already been there for an hour. We need to leave pronto!" She pulls me toward the door.

"Emmie, will you keep an eye on things? I'll be right back!"

"You bet. Just go!" Emmie waves us off just as Macy catches up to us.

My sister links her arm to mine. "The two of you aren't having fun without me. Georgie and I will go on one of those haunted hayrides while you wrestle with the perpetrator."

"I've been dying to go on that haunted hayride," I say.

Macy shrugs. "Well, if you're lucky, she'll kill you and you can haunt the ride yourself."

"You're not funny."

I'm pretty sure Sarah Abernathy isn't the killer.

But her husband?

He's another haunted story altogether.

CHAPTER 16

A canopy of thick, dark clouds hangs heavy over the Haunted Harvest Festival.

Both Macy and Georgie pull their coats tight as we brave the chill while making our way into the thick of the festival. There's a midway rife with games and adorable stuffed pumpkins of every shape and size as prizes, along with stuffed ghosts and witches and goblins and scarecrows. The line for hot apple cider is long enough to make you think twice, and I note the pumpkin patch is beginning to look scarce of its cheery orange globes as the month wears on.

I've brought both Sherlock and Peanut with me, as a sort of double-barreled ammunition. Dogs are typically considered to be *chick* magnets—and that will be great if I can get one chick in particular to magnetize toward me—Sarah, and if not her, I'm really hoping her boys will be drawn to them, and perfectly distracted while I grill their mother on whether or not their father could be a killer.

Sherlock tugs at the leash. ***There's a giant cat over there, and it's grinning at me, Bizzy! I think it's eating children by the dozen.***

I glance to where his nose is pointed, and sure enough there just so happens to be a giant bounce house in the shape of a black cat currently being enjoyed by what looks like far too many children.

Peanut barks at the oversized balloon. *Kids are screaming and trying to hop on out! We need to rescue them, Bizzy. Let's go now.*

"Now that's quite a bounce house," I say to the paranoid pooches while trying not to sound like an insane person to my sister. Georgie knows all about my so-called insanity, and she often begs me to tell her what the animals are thinking.

Macy moans as a kid walks by holding a candy apple that looks as if it were rolled in marshmallows and chocolate covered candies in a rainbow of colors.

"I need one of those devilish treats in my stomach like yesterday." Macy plucks off her white knit gloves. "Who's in?"

"*Me!*" Georgie wails while raising her hand to the sky. "Oh, I want twelve. They're so adorable. And that way I can have a few for later." She winks my way. "I'm hoping a very special trick-or-treater will haunt my halls on Halloween Eve. I plan on picking me up one of those rich hotties at the party Saturday night and taking him home with me. And all I have to feed company is broken glass."

Macy grunts, "I've met the men you've brought back to your place, Georgie. I'm pretty sure they survive off a steady diet of broken glass."

Georgie makes a face. "More like broken hearts."

Macy cinches her purse over her shoulder. "We'll catch you later, Bizzy. We're going to stuff our faces before we puke it all up on the hayride. Try not to end up dead. It's going to be murder rounding up the dogs in this crowd, and I'm sort of growing attached to the little one."

I wrinkle my nose at my cheeky sister. "I'll do my best to keep breathing. Keep your phones on just in case."

They take off running—literally.

Apparently, you're never too old to race to the candy apple

stand. But, in their defense, they are gourmet candy apples and I'm eyeing them myself.

Sherlock leads the way to the bounce house, both agitated and excited to see what all the screaming is about.

"No biting, no barking," I sing. "Remember, they're just little boys. They like to play as much as you do."

Peanut wags his tail and tongue. *I hope they're just as big as Fish. I like to catch her between my paws.*

"I'm guessing they're a little bit bigger than that."

I stop cold as I spot a group of mothers gathered just shy of the bounce house, and I recognize the blonde with a pixie cut from the pictures of Luke and his bride on the internet. Her face is set in a scowl as she listens to the other women in her circle.

A child slips out of the giant cat's maw, and two of the mothers run in that direction.

Now it's just Sarah and a younger girl who looks bored silly sitting next to her.

I make my way over.

"Hey," I say as I point to the bale of hay to the left of them. "Mind if I take a seat?"

The younger girl stands. "Go right ahead. I was just about to get something to eat." *Like six of those candy apples. If I see another one go by, I'm liable to pluck it right out of a stranger's hand.* "You want anything, Sarah?"

"No"—the blonde smiles up at her—"but I'll watch the girls for you."

Oh, thank goodness. The girl gives a friendly wave. *A minute without the kids. I think I'll buy myself a bouquet of churros to celebrate.*

Perfect.

I take a seat right next to Sarah, and Sherlock pops up next to me, demanding her attention.

I like this one, Bizzy. Sherlock whimpers and pants while blinking those large brown eyes at her.

Peanut wiggles his way into the mix and wags his stubby little tail back and forth until the two of us share a laugh.

Sarah's whole face brightens at the sight of the friendly dogs I've schlepped along for the ride.

"Well, aren't the two of you handsome." She gives both Sherlock and Peanut a quick pat on the head. "Are they boys? I just assume everything is a male these days. I have twin boys, so my world is pretty blue." She laughs and I can't help but note how pretty and sweet she seems. There's an air of innocence about her that some people just seem to exude and she's definitely one of them.

"That they are. This is Sherlock and that's Peanut. They're friendly, too. So I'm sure they wouldn't mind your boys one bit."

"Good thing." She gives a wistful shake of the head. "As soon as my boys spot them, these puppies are pretty much doomed."

"My husband loves dogs, too," I say, lying through my teeth about having one of those matrimonially bound creatures. For a brief moment, I envision myself walking down the aisle of Cider Cove Covenant Church and seeing Jasper looking lethally handsome in a three-piece suit. Every last bit of me demands that my imagination races ahead to the wedding night, but I'm quick to shake all thoughts of the dapper detective out of my head. "How about your husband?"

"My husband?" She blinks back as if the idea of having a husband were a joke—and it just might be to her.

Before she can answer, a couple of little blond boys bound over, screaming as they tackle both Sherlock and Peanut to the ground.

Bizzy! Sherlock sounds as if he's laughing, and he certainly looks as if he's having a good time while rolling on his back.

Peanut howls and pants and he spins in a circle, chasing his tail while one of the boys does his best to catch him.

"What was I saying?" Sarah shakes her head as a laugh bubbles from her. "Oh, my husband." Her expression grows flat as she glowers into the crowd. "Not everyone hits the lottery with one of those. I guess it's sort of hit-and-miss." She shrugs as she looks to her happy little sons. "But Luke does try." A shiver runs up my spine once she says his name. "He's working two jobs, so we hardly ever see each other. Sometimes I wonder if he's got a whole other life going on. His work has him traveling, so we don't get to spend every night together. And, of course, he works late weekends, too. I made a joke the other day that I would have to introduce him to the boys at some point," she huffs. "It would be funny if it weren't true. But then again, nobody said having twins was easy. We weren't exactly rolling in money when we found out. I try to buy secondhand whenever I can, but kids are so expensive regardless. I was waitressing when I met Luke, but the cost of childcare is so much it didn't make sense for me to leave them once they were born."

"Kids do seem like a huge responsibility. I can hardly keep up with my pets, so I can imagine how much more challenging a person—two of them—would be."

"Oh, pets are a cakewalk compared to kids. Are you and your husband trying yet?"

"Trying what?" I blink over at her, completely oblivious until it hits me like a baby bottle right between the eyes. And then for the briefest of moments, I envision Jasper holding a tiny swaddled bundle in his arms, and I'm right back to swooning for that man. I bet Jasper will make a wonderful father.

Sarah belts out a hearty laugh. "Trying for *kids*. But I guess you're not there yet. Some of the girls I know get really into it. It's sort of fun—watching your cycle, stealing your husband away for baby time. But you better watch out. You could always end up like me. *Twins*." She grimaces as she says it. "My father likes to joke we were trying too hard."

My heart breaks just hearing her talk about her family. If her father knew what Luke was doing behind her back, I'm sure he'd try to kill him.

"My husband is a lot like yours," I say. "A real worker bee. Sometimes my mind wanders and I start to think he really *is* living a double life. I mean, I would never know it. He's always out—some nights he just doesn't come home. It makes me wonder what he's capable of. What kinds of dark things he might be doing." A rumble of thunder goes off up above, and it's as if all life at the Haunted Harvest Festival stops for a moment.

Sarah shudders as she stares vacantly into the crowd.

"Luke has a dark side." The muscles in her jaw redefine themselves as if she were angry about it. "He's shown it to me before. It's part of the reason I don't complain too much about him not being home. I don't want the boys to see it."

A chill runs through me. Sarah seems convinced Luke has a dark side. Luke certainly had a secret—and I bet he was hiding it from both Shelby and Sarah.

A thought comes to me. Chelsea mentioned that Luke had done something very bad and Shelby just found out about it that night. And Luke mentioned that Sarah had contacted Shelby in the middle of the seminar. Shelby was very angry with him. Anyone could see that. Luke knew his cushy ride at Harris Financial would be over.

Luke had a very big motive to kill poor Shelby.

I look down at the squealing boys as they wrestle with Sherlock and Peanut.

Luke had two very big motives to keep Shelby quiet.

A couple of mothers head this way with their kids in tow and Sarah wrangles her boys together.

"It was nice meeting you," she says. "You know, I actually feel a lot better after talking to you. It's weird, isn't it? Sometimes you need to say things out loud to know what direction you're going to take next in life." She leans in my way. "Let's just say, my husband and I are about to have a very big talk. Good luck with yours."

She takes off, and I look out at the crowd as the skies grow ever darker. The air grows with a crisp fall snap to it and demands that I cinch my coat.

I have a feeling Luke Parker—*Abernathy*—wanted to make sure Shelby didn't stand in his way. He had a very big secret to keep from his wife. And he might have made sure that Shelby would keep it forever.

I need another chance to speak with Luke. I think I'd better make sure Luke knows he's invited to Ginger's Halloween Monster Mash.

And unfortunately, I have a feeling there really will be a very real monster in our midst.

CHAPTER 17

$\mathcal{H}$alloween is officially on Tuesday, but this Saturday night at the Country Cottage Inn we're determined to give that haunted evening a wicked run for its money—or *candy* as it were.

"Jordy, this place looks amazing!" I pull him in by the arm and give him a squeeze. I'm dressed as a fairy in an ultra-short lime green dress and tiny glittery wings strapped to my back. I'll admit, I look less preschool and more reform school with a naughty flair, but I couldn't resist. It's adorable.

We're standing just outside of the ballroom where the courtyard and the woods that lie just beyond that are decorated to the hilt with what seems like hundreds of glowing pumpkins. Each one of them wears a unique face, some cute, some scary, and some of the happy orange globes simply have holes bore into them. But each and every one looks absolutely magical.

"Jordy, it's breathtaking."

"Thanks. Check that out." He nods to the woods where the trees are lit up with enough lavender twinkle lights to give the entire Western Hemisphere a haunted appeal. "We put cobwebs between the trees to keep the crowd from getting too far into the woods."

"Webbed fencing. Now there's something original."

"The woods look friendly enough, but we both know you can get disoriented in minutes and end up miles in the wrong direction trying to find your way out."

"I agree. It's a haunted maze without even trying." An odd sight catches my eye—a large pot brimming with pumpkins. "Why is that planter sitting right in the middle of the walkway?"

Jordy winces. He's dressed as a football player—wearing his high school jersey and sweats. He's even donned a swath of black grease under each eye in an effort to go the extra mile.

"That's where the body was," he whispers. "It sort of felt sacred. I didn't want anyone trampling that area."

"Jordy, that's so kind. Thank you for being so thoughtful. I'll admit, it is a little heartbreaking being out here." An icy breeze whistles by. "I'm really impressed by you tonight. And I have to say, I'm impressed by something else. You're usually the last person to dress up for a Halloween party. I'm glad to see you getting into the haunted spirit of things."

"Thanks, Biz. I'm hoping to impress someone else tonight, too." He glances to the glowing entry to our right as a crowd of bodies begins to circulate inside. *I bet she's in there. She probably won't remember me. And who the heck cares?* He takes a deep breath. *I guess I do.*

"Jordy." I tug him back by the wrist. "Whoever this girl is, she must be pretty special to have grabbed your attention. Take it from your ex-wife, you deserve someone special."

We share a warm laugh before heading on in.

The grand ballroom at the Country Cottage Inn has been transformed into a bona fide haunted house with its orange twinkle lights, glowing pumpkins dotting the refreshments tables with their toothless smiles, and chandeliers laden with spider webs that drip down and blow about like poltergeists with the slightest breeze. There's a DJ playing a rather spooktacular playlist, and the masses that have already poured into the room are all dressed up in every costume known to man.

The women all look as if they're some racy version of a nurse, a princess, or a witch. And the men run the gamut from vampires to lumberjacks. I give a quick look around the vicinity for Ginger King. Her book signing table is set up in the back, but she's yet to arrive. And in truth, she's only about ten minutes late. I'd better head to the front desk and let Grady know to lead her straight to the ballroom when she arrives.

I thread my way through the room just as Emmie heads this way balancing a couple of platters brimming with her pumpkin spice mini muffins. She's dressed as a flapper in a short black dress with elongated fringes that bounce to life with her every step. She's donned a long pearl necklace that loops tightly around her neck just once and the rest of it dangles to her belly. There's a feathered headband strapped to her head that sparkles and catches the light and gives her an overall enchanted feel.

"I'll get these to the dessert table," she calls out as we pass one another. "You make an adorable Tink!"

"Says the sexy flapper! You can teach me to do the Charleston in an hour."

I speed to the foyer where the noise level is dampened, but the excitement is just as high. Last night, Grady and I stayed late, stretching spider webs all over the reception counter and adding even more pumpkins and ghosts to the mix.

Sherlock and Peanut are seated right up front, looking beyond adorable in their costumes. Sherlock is dressed as a giant goldfish—a sight that Fish has not stopped laughing at. And I bought Peanut a penguin costume that actually makes him look as if he's a standing upright and waddling when you look at him from the front. They're both so hilarious people haven't stopped snapping pictures of them all day.

Sherlock bounds my way. *Bizzy, next year I'd like to be a superhero. The kind Jasper watches on TV.*

I can't help but laugh. "I think you're already a superhero, Sherlock."

Grady does a double take this way. He's dressed as Spiderman sans the face mask and he looks adorable as if he's in his pj's. "Have I ever told you I think it's cute the way you talk to the animals as if they can understand you?"

"I can't help it. A part of me really does believe they can."

Peanut barks as if acknowledging this. *I like my costume, Bizzy. It makes people smile. Georgie laughed so hard she said she needed to wear a diaper around me.*

I grimace at the thought. "Georgie is one step away from wearing one all the time."

Fish hops up onto the granite counter and lets out a yodeling meow. *Bizzy Baker, you get this ridiculous hat off of me, right this minute.*

I bite down hard on my lower lip to keep from laughing.

"Fish, you make the cutest pirate on the face of the planet," I say, adjusting the miniature black pirate's hat I've strapped to her head. She's wearing a costume that drapes down the front and secures to her front paws, a red and white striped shirt attached to a pair of stuffed jeans. There's a pair of stuffed arms poking out of the shirt portion, and in one hand she's holding a tiny sword as if she were readying to attack. It's so comical to look at her. Everyone who has seen her has done a double take before bursting out with laughter.

I'm only wearing this for you, Bizzy, Fish growls. *Just remember, you promised an extra helping of my Fancy Beast dinner.*

"And I plan on rewarding all three of you for being such good sports," I say just as an all too familiar witch and scarecrow head this way.

"Dad?" My eyes enlarge at the sight of his hand caressing Gwyneth's back.

She's wearing a loose black dress with a large pointy hat planted over her head and a sparkly wand in her hand.

Why do I get the feeling this is a familiar uniform for her that she's worn before on a far less celebrated occasion—say, a full moon in the presence of her coven?

Dad, however, looks as if he went hog wild at the Montgomerys' pumpkin patch and stuffed his jeans and flannel with hay. He's donned a ratty old wicker hat and painted his nose a cheery shade of orange.

"Bizzy Bizzy." He gives Sherlock a quick scratch. "This is one good-looking crew. We'll catch you inside."

Gwyneth sneers at me as she leads the way and, just like that, they're off.

"That might be the scariest thing I see all night," I say to Grady just as Macy trots over in a pair of sky-high heels, her hair done in tight kinky curls, and she's wearing a low-cut, tight-fitted red dress. "Well, if it isn't the devil herself," I tease.

"Oh, hush." Macy pauses a moment to adjust her burgeoning décolleté. "I'm not wearing a costume."

"I didn't say you were."

She offers a wry smile before leaning in. "I'd gift you a special finger, but there's a gentleman in our midst." She nods his way. "Hello, Grady. I'll see you both inside. Ta-ta for now." She scampers off, and Grady gives a dark gurgle of a laugh.

"Macy is gunning for one of those rich men, isn't she?"

"I don't know what she's gunning for," I say. "And my guess is, neither does she."

Chelsea Ashley steps in with a rather dapper looking man by her side, and my stomach sinks a moment at the sight of them.

"Chelsea"—I say, trying my best to sound bright and cheery— "and Carter O'Riley."

Chelsea is dressed as a vamped-up Little Red Riding Hood, and Carter has a light smattering of face makeup on that gives him the appearance of a furry yet comely wolf.

She's staring at us. Chelsea frowns for a moment. *I knew we'd be judged for it. But Shelby is gone. That means all girl code is off the table and it's open season on Carter. Besides, someone has to help him get over poor Shelby. Not that he ever will. And not that I ever will—but that's the one commonality we'll have. How much we loved her.*

I head over and offer a friendly smile. "The two of you look spectacular!"

"Really?" Chelsea's face fills with relief.

"Yes, really. I wish I would have thought of that. I don't even know what my own boyfriend will show up as." I cringe for a moment since I all but accused them of dating.

Carter gives a cheery laugh. "Well, Chels and I are new. We're sort of feeling our way around to see where things might lead. Right now, it's grief that's bonding us." *And it's a hell of a bond. My heart aches, but Chelsea somehow makes things better.*

"I think that's very sweet," I say.

A group of men walk in and give a howl of approval to their fearless leader.

"I'd better brief these guys on how to behave." Carter offers a quick wave my way. "I'll see you both inside."

He stalks off in their direction just as Chelsea coos at the sight of Fish.

"I had a cat just like this when I was a kid." She gives Fish a gentle pat on the back before snapping a picture of her. Chelsea looks my way. "Any word on Nessa?" She winces. "I can't believe she'd do something like that."

"I don't think she did, but the wrap is sticking and I don't like it." It takes all of my effort not to clap my hand over my mouth, but it's too late. The words have already spilled out. I'm pretty sure if I went to detective school, the first thing they'd teach would be not to let all your cards show. "Chelsea, can I ask you something?"

"Sure." She glances past me as the crowd grows increasingly

boisterous, and I can feel my window with her quickly closing. "I heard you were arrested for shoplifting a few years back." I offer a guilty shrug. "I also heard you took the blame for something you didn't do."

Her eyes widen in horror. "Who told you that?"

"A little bird." Called the internet. "Anyway, I just thought something like that would weigh heavy on a person, and I wanted to say I'm sorry you went through it."

She closes her eyes and takes a deep breath. "Thank you, Bizzy. It was hell. It was the darkest time in my life. I was raised to follow every single law in the book. I would never even think of doing something like that. So when I was busted for something I didn't do, it stung all the more." Her lips quiver like she might cry. *And now Shelby is dead and I'll have to bear the weight of her sins forever. I wish Shelby were still here. I know eventually I could have convinced her to tell the truth. But now I can't. I guess you could say, that in a sense, the killer has hurt me, too.*

"I'd better get in." She nods to the ballroom. "I'll see you inside, Bizzy."

And just like that, Chelsea Ashley is wiped off my suspect list.

Scout Pratt bounds over with her body squeezed into a rather sultry, fitted green velvet skirt with a shiny tail attached to it. She's wearing a bra made of twin oversized seashells and her hair is dyed a shocking shade of red.

"Well, aren't you the merry mermaid," I say as I take her in. "You look fabulous."

She makes a face. "I don't feel so fabulous. Ginger wants me to head into the room and make sure the DJ gives her a proper welcome." She pauses a moment to give Peanut and Sherlock a quick pat. "You're so lucky that your co-workers are cute and have very little to say."

I give a warm laugh. "They have more to say than you think."

Scout picks up Peanut and gives him a kiss. "I bet this poor guy misses his mama."

That I do, Peanut whimpers.

"That he does," I'm quick to translate for him.

"Poor Shelby." Scout's expression falls flat. "I mean, we definitely had our troubles." *She was an outright witch to me, but I would never disparage her in front of this cute little guy.* Scout kisses Peanut on the forehead before placing him back down.

"Believe me, I get it. I have people in my life that I don't get along with, but that doesn't mean I want to see them dead."

No sooner do the words leave my lips than Camila traipses down the stairs in a black latex bustier, a pair of black fishnets, and a sexy mask slipped over her eyes that gives her that cat's eye effect. Come to think of it, that's probably why she's wearing the long black tail and tiny pink triangular ears. Camila has dressed herself like the sex kitten she is, and I can't help but frown.

She looks stunning. She looks beyond stunning.

And with her perfectly pouty features and wavy long hair, she looks as if she belongs in a calendar. A greasy calendar for men. One that I have a feeling every breathing male on the planet would approve of once that calendar comes out.

She averts her eyes once she spots me and heads out front. Most likely to pounce on Jasper.

I sigh as I look to Scout. "Do you think now that Shelby is gone, you can find it in you to forgive her for whatever misgivings the two of you had?"

Scout glances past me. "I can forgive her. Now that she's gone, it all almost seems trivial." *Almost. Shelby could be wicked to the bone when she wanted to be. Lord knows I had every reason to want her gone. But then, Nessa did the dirty work for me, and I get to breathe a sigh of relief and go on with the rest of my life.*

My mouth opens and I take a quick breath. Scout didn't do it. But she had a strong motive. It could have easily been her.

Scout leans in. "One thing that I learned from Shelby is that you should curate who you bring into your life. Not everyone is looking out for your best intentions." A crowd bustles by and we scoot out of the way. "I better get inside before Ginger shows up." She looks to the door and shudders. *Now, if only the killer would come back and aim for Ginger.* She makes a face. *A terrible thought, I know. But she is a monster. There is no doubt about it.*

Scout takes off and I take a few steps toward the front, admiring the silk maple leaves enwreathing the double door entry lit up with tiny orange lights. Jordy stacked pumpkins to the right and left of the entry, along with a couple of witches' brooms dipped in cinnamon oil that adds a heavenly scent to the entire inn. It's all so homey, it makes me wish October would last forever.

A shockingly handsome vampire steps into view and sends my heart ratcheting up to unsafe levels. I'm about to wrap arms around him and offer up a big, juicy kiss when I see my mother strapped to his side looking every bit the naughty nurse. Her face is powdered bone white, and she has a trail of blood dripping from the seam of her lip.

"Mom? Max!" My heart lurches as if it were still unsure if it should be thumping so hard for this Jasper look-alike. "You both look downright frightening. I can honestly say you scared me." For far different reasons than they imagine.

I will never get used to seeing my mother with a knockoff of my very own boyfriend. My stomach sinks because I'm still holding out hope that Jasper and I will solidify that teeny, tiny, all-important detail sometime soon.

Max laughs, exposing a pair of fangs that look as if they're bona fide extensions of his real teeth. "Ree showed up at my restaurant today and passed out candy to all the little kids. Her, they loved. Me? Let's just say they were twitching for the nearest crucifix."

Mom pulls him in close. "Oh, hush." She shakes her head my way. "He's a hot vampire and he knows it."

Max waggles his brows. "A hot vampire looking to get lucky with an even hotter nurse."

They share a sharp cackle as they head over toward the ballroom.

I have a feeling if those two stick, it will make for a very long life filled with blatant innuendos that happen to involve my mother.

At least she's got good taste in men.

I turn back toward the peachy glow of the entry when my heart stops cold.

Clad in black with a long leather jacket, a rather ornate buckle over his dark jeans, and a puffy black dress shirt with equally ornate silver buttons is a heart-stoppingly handsome homicide detective from the Seaview Sheriff's Department.

"I don't know who you are, but if you still happen to have a pair of handcuffs on you, please arrest me and drag me off to your place."

A growl of a laugh comes from Jasper as he pulls me in. He lifts his left hand to reveal a stump with a hook attached to it.

"Argh," I say. "You're Captain Hook."

His eyes ride up and down my lime green dress. "And I do believe I've found my Tinker Bell. Peter Pan doesn't stand a chance." He steals a quick kiss just as a hurricane of a redhead stampedes her way inside the foyer, effectively dislodging me from Jasper.

"Oh, good. It's you, Bizzy." Ginger rushes to the reception area and I dutifully follow along. "Please put my things below the counter for me." She shoves her purse and a tote bag my way.

"Sure thing," I say, handing them to Grady and he does just that. I give the panting diva a quick once-over. "Wow, Ginger. You look like a million dollars." And she does. Ginger has on a gold sequin gown that catches the light and glitters with her every move. Her hair is styled in tight little ringlets around her neck, her makeup is glammed up and perfectly vampy with bright red lipstick, and there's even a dark mole colored in on her left cheek. And in one hand she has a bouquet of ruby red roses that, for some reason, pulls her entire over-the-top glamorous look together.

"I should look like a million dollars." She sniffs the flowers in her hand and makes a face. "This dress is a Verragamo original and it costs more than my first car. I'm an A-lister, tonight and every night." She gives a little wink. "I'm supposed to be a movie star." She wags the bouquet my way.

"Well, you're set to shine tonight," I say. "All of your books were delivered yesterday and I had them stacked around your table. Scout is there now, taking care of everything for you."

She rolls her eyes. *There's another idiot I have to deal with.* "Hopefully, she didn't give any copies away like she did last time. That girl costs me more money than she's worth. In fact, don't ruin her surprise, but tonight is her last night. I can't take any more of her buffoonery. Hey"—her eyes widen my way—"you're not looking for another job, are you?"

"Not yet. But thank you for the offer." I think. I'm about to say something else when I spot a certain sultry sex kitten cozying up with a drop-dead gorgeous pirate who just so happens to belong to me.

Ginger follows my gaze and growls, "As if she stands a chance. I'll hook that man by the end of the night." Her lips bleed a wicked smile. "Just you wait and see."

She takes off for the ballroom while I openly scowl at Jasper and the all too friendly feline attempting to use his body like a scratching post.

Jasper seems to be backing up and saying something to her all at the same time. He gives a casual glance my way and does a quick double take with that deer in the headlights look in his eyes. He steadies Camila a moment with his hand and says something to her before making his way over.

Sherlock growls, *Should I bite him, Bizzy? Should I?*

"Maybe." I whisper, only half-teasing.

"Bizzy." Jasper sheds his signature grin as he examines me

from head to foot. "You are gorgeous beyond belief. Have I ever told you I have a thing for green fairies?"

A wry smile breaks free on my lips. "No, but lucky for you, I have a very real thing for pirates."

"I hope you don't mind." Jasper closes his eyes a moment. "But I think this is the perfect time."

I suck in a quick breath. "To break things off with me?" The words leave my lips before I have the chance to process them.

"No." His head inches back in dismay. "To have that talk with Camila. You know, the one that makes it clear that I'm off the market and we will never be anything more than friends." He winces. "And to be honest, *friends* is a very strong word."

"Oh, right." I can feel my cheeks heat. So Jasper is unavailable? A silly grin floats to my lips. "Take all the time you need. I've got my hands full for the next few hours anyway. I'll catch you inside."

Jasper nods as he heads her way, and together they leave through the front door. They look perfectly suited for one another. A beautiful yin to his handsome yang, and it sours my stomach for a second. I know for a fact Camila isn't going down without a fight.

But before I can dwell on it too long, a real monster arrives to the party.

And I'd bet all the candy corn in Cider Cove that I'm looking right at the killer.

CHAPTER 18

*L*uke Parker darkens the doorway with his blond hair swept heavily to one side. He's donned a T-shirt and jeans and he looks far more youthful than he does on a normal day.

"Hey, Luke." It takes everything in me to sound chipper as I greet him.

He's a two-timer. The very worst kind of a two-timer—one with a wife and two beautiful twin boys. "I'm glad you decided to make it out tonight."

The Monster Mash is just getting underway, and already there are far too many costumed bodies pressing their way in the direction of the ballroom.

He shrugs, giving the place a quick sweep. "Thought I'd check it out. I guess the party's that way."

"It sure is. In fact, I'm heading that way. What are you supposed to be this evening?" I try to freeze a smile onto my face, but it doesn't seem to be working. Luke had the strongest motive to keep Shelby quiet. And now she'll never tell anyone what she found out just before she died.

Luke was frantic that night—with the exact kind of paranoia that can push someone over the edge.

"Boy band." He shrugs. "Just one member." His chest bounces with a dull laugh. "Shelby always said that's what she liked about me best." He slaps his cheek lightly. "My boyish face."

"Well, you do have an adorable factor about you." I snarl without meaning to. "I bet you'll be snapped up by some beautiful girl soon enough. Men like you don't stay on the market very long."

What? He shoots a wide-eyed look my way. *Is she hitting on me?*

A breath hitches in my throat just as we enter the ballroom and I spot Deputy Leo Granger with a vixen strapped to his side and I quickly pluck him my way, sending the vixen flying. It's not until I glance back do I realize the vixen in question was Mayor Mack Woods looking every bit like her true witchy self.

Really, Leo? I shake my head at him.

"Luke, you remember my boyfriend, Leo." I glance over at my faux suitor to find he's dressed exactly like a deputy. Perfect. Nothing like a Glock strapped to your side to make a prospective suspect want to suddenly flee the scene.

Luke nods over at him. "Hey." He shakes Leo's hand. "How's the boat shopping going?" He washes him with a quick glance. "Cool costume, by the way. Looks real."

"Thanks." Leo's chest expands with pride. With his dark hair and dark, mysterious eyes I can see why Mack has suddenly glommed onto him.

Speaking of the witch...

Mack pops up again. "We were just about to dance, Bizzy," she grits the words through her teeth. With that black lipstick and that powder green face, her teeth look so bright they could glow in the dark. She's donned a short black dress cut to ragged strips around the hem and silver tights that make her legs shimmer like night magic. It's safe to say, Mack is a beauty queen no matter what putrid shade her face happens to be.

Leo gives a wistful shake of the head. I thought so myself. He gives a quick wink as she stalks off to the dance floor with him.

"Easy come, easy go." I shrug over at Luke and I make a face as soon as I realize how tasteless that was. "Please excuse my crass remark. In no way did I mean—"

He waves it off. "Trust me. It's fine. I know what you meant."

The lights dim and a drumroll takes over.

The DJ taps the mic as he garners the attention of everyone in the room.

"Welcome, guys and ghouls!" The DJs voice echoes and vibrates over the walls. "Kicking off tonight's festivities is the royalty who knows exactly how to land the man of any woman's dream, Ginger King." The room explodes in hoots and hollers as a riotous applause breaks out. "She'll be signing books, and giving looks, at the table in the back. We hope you enjoy the music and the food. If you're single, be sure to mingle. Eat, dance, stay late, and have a safe time."

An upbeat tune bounces through the speakers, a notch louder than it was before, and half the room is gyrating to the rhythm.

Ginger takes her place at the book signing table, and soon enough a line snakes around the periphery of the room—mostly women, but there are a smattering of men, too.

"She's popular," I say.

"That she is." Luke purses his lips. *And I bet she's drowning in dollars. Ginger's given me the look before, so I know she's interested. She didn't care if Shelby was around. She wanted it. I could have jumped on the chance. Heck, maybe I could have really given them something to bicker about.*

My blood boils just listening to his sickening thoughts. Now that he's knocked Shelby out of the way, all he can think about is where his next sugar mama will come from.

"Luke"—I block Ginger from his line of vision—"I think Leo is cheating on me."

"What?" He inches back with wild eyes. *This chick is certifiable.*

"No, it's true. I think he's seeing some woman in Whaler's Cove. Why do men do it? What makes them cheat?"

Whaler's Cove? He takes in a long, soothing breath as if reliving a memory. *That's where I met Shelby. I had it hot for teacher, all right.* He cranes his neck as he looks at Ginger. *And I have it hot for her student, too.*

He looks back my way. "Men cheat." He shrugs it off as if it were no big deal. *Get over it, lady.* "My dad did it. My brothers do it."

"But why? Isn't one woman enough to satisfy you?"

"It's not that." He gives a long blink before stepping to the side to study Ginger. "Different women fulfill different roles."

"Just like Shelby filled a role in your life?"

Luke's lips part as he looks my way. "I know what you're thinking. I know what everyone is thinking. That I don't deserve that job at Harris Financial."

"No, Luke." My heart thumps wildly. "What I'm thinking is that Shelby was very upset the night she was killed."

"Darn right, she was," he says, shooting a dark look in Ginger's direction.

My goodness, it's as if he's suddenly hypnotized by her. Sure, she makes a glamorous movie star, but can he not focus on the task at hand for a single moment?

I try to block his view of her. "What do you think she was upset about? I mean, clearly you knew what you were doing at the finance company. You gave Leo and me the right forms." That might be true, but I'm not above rubbing his ego to get a confession out of him.

"I did." His brows furrow. "And I think I deserve to stick around." *And with Shelby gone, I will. Her old man caved to my pleas. And now he thinks it's exactly what Shelby would have wanted as well.*

Luke might be dressed like a one-man boy band, but he's a snake through and through.

"Luke"—I say, trying to pull him out of his Ginger King stupor once again—"what do you think had Shelby all worked up that night? I bumped into her in the foyer and she said it had something to do with you."

His eyes twitch my way again as bodies crush us from every side.

I'm not sure how many people have filed into the room, but I'm guessing the fire code is about to be tapped.

"She was angry with me. Okay? We were having a fight over something stupid." He tries to get a better look at Ginger, and I step in front of him again.

"She said something about a *wife*," I lie through my teeth and don't mind at all. "What do you think she meant?"

His Adam's apple rises and falls. "I don't know. But it's not important anymore." His entire body sags. "That wife sent her husband packing."

A small gasp emits from me.

Luke glowers into the crowd a moment. *Sarah gave me the boot and I thought it'd feel like a relief. She said she met some angel at the pumpkin patch who gave her perfect clarity.* He rolls his eyes. *I bet it was some dude. Here I thought I was the only player in the family. Go figure.* He lets out a hard breath. *If Shelby had lived, we could have had something real. I know it.*

"Look"—his gaze falls to mine—"I'm not like my dad or my brothers. Not anymore. I'm sorry about your boyfriend. I hope it works out for the two of you. I really do. But I need to get in that line before Ginger runs out of books—and looks. Wish me luck."

Luke gazes over at Ginger as he heads that way. *Maybe this one won't die or walk out on me.*

"Bizzy!" Georgie comes at me with a couple of pooches in

tow and a tiny pirate hat bobbing in the background. Her long gray hair is flying every which way and she's got an ear-to-ear grin. "This is magic! I vote we have a Monster Mash every weekend."

"That might turn me into a monster," I say, looking back at Luke. His thoughts sure didn't sound very guilty, but then, sociopaths are incapable of feeling anything.

Fish entwines herself between my ankles. *And I vote we never have a Halloween again.*

Sherlock gives a spastic glance in every direction at once. *Where's the bacon, Bizzy? Where's the bacon?*

"I'm afraid I don't have any bacon on me, Sherlock." I shrug down his way.

Georgie waves me off. "Ignore her. Both you and Peanut will get plenty of bacon. Stick with me, kids. I know how to have some real fun."

I give her orange and black kaftan an approving once-over. She has on an arm full of bangles, large hoop earrings, and enough necklaces to sink a battleship.

"What are you supposed to be, Georgie?"

"I'm a hippy artist." She snaps her fingers up near her ears. "What do you think?"

"I think you're a hippy artist every day. And I think you make a darn good one."

"You bet I do, sister." She bumps her hip to mine. "Come on, friends! It's time to show these kids a real fright on the dance floor." She takes off and immediately starts a conga line in the process. Leave it to Georgie to be the life of the party.

Too bad I don't feel like partying at the moment.

Close to an hour drifts by as I watch Luke slowly making progress in the book line until he finally gets his turn at bat with Ginger. She all but throws a book at him and sends him on his way—and he doesn't look too happy about it either.

Luke looks fit to be tied for all of ten seconds before a sultry temptress dressed as a mermaid catches his eye and he heads on over.

Luke seems just fine bouncing from one woman to another. He does seem rather easygoing. Ginger all but slapped him in the face with that book she wrote.

Something in me lurches.

That's it!

I know who the killer is, without a shadow of a doubt.

CHAPTER 19

*T*he crowd at the Monster Mash grows increasingly boisterous with each passing minute. And it looks as if the person I'm tracking has had quite enough of the party themselves—at least for the moment.

I thread my way through the thicket of bodies until I hit the cool exterior of the courtyard and I step on out into the crisp fall air. Night has fallen hard, and it's virtually empty out here, save for the hundreds of jack-o-lanterns glowing and flickering, giving the night the haunted appeal it deserves.

Sherlock, Peanut, and Fish scuttle out behind me, but my gaze is unbreakable from the sight before me.

Standing next to the makeshift shrine Jordy placed over the very spot where Shelby Harris breathed her last breath is the very last person I would have suspected. But I should have. The truth was there before me all along.

She places a single red rose over the large pot brimming with pumpkins of every size.

"Ginger?" I whisper her name as I come upon her and she spins on her heels. Her dress glitters purple under the duress of the lavender twinkle lights, and everything about Ginger King is a bewitching sight.

"*Bizzy*," she hisses my name like a reprimand. Her eyes flit to the furry creatures surrounding me and she looks as if she's about to be sick.

Is it her, Bizzy? Is it? Sherlock dances left then right, alive with nervous energy.

Fish lets out a ferocious meow and Ginger lifts a brow her way. But Peanut scuttles off toward the woods, whimpering and whining as if he were afraid she was about to chuck her shoe at him—something I have no doubt she's done before. She's capable of far worse.

"You put a flower over the very spot where Shelby was killed," I say the words so low I wonder if she's heard them.

Ginger sniffs hard, her eyes glinting with tears. "That's right. Shelby and I were friends."

"You were friends. You were very close friends, weren't you?"

She glances out at the woods lit up like a supernatural wonderland. "Some might say too close."

"You did a lot together." I take in a steady breath, trying my best not to spook her. "You were good friends. She let you borrow her dog to make you more affable to the crowds."

She gags as if the thought offended her. "I never cared if anyone liked me, let alone because I was holding some silly little dog," Ginger grunts as she plucks the rose back from where she laid it and tosses it to the ground, grinding her shoe over the bloom as if she were putting out a cigarette.

Fish runs up to get a better look at the floral malfeasance, and she looks adorably like a miniature pirate ready to wreak havoc with that tiny sword stitched to her costume.

Did you see that, Bizzy? Fish twitches her head my way. **She just killed that flower—the same way I bet she killed Shelby.**

I clear my throat. "Shelby was a great writer, wasn't she? I heard she helped teach English at Whaler's Cove Community

College a while back. I bet she gave you great input on your book."

Her eyes widen a notch. Her lips pull down, giving her that beauty queen gone feral look.

I take a steady breath. "Luke said there was something going on between you and Shelby. Is that what it was? The book?"

She blinks hard as if she were trying her best to look affronted. However, according to her clenched fists, she looks angry.

"Excuse me?" She squints over at me. "Are you trying to imply something about my writing?" *What in the heck is happening here? Does this nitwit think she's about to outsmart me?*

"I'm not implying anything about your writing," I say. "The other day in the café when we were discussing the party, you mentioned that you couldn't write your way out of a paper bag."

Her mouth rounds out. "Oh, *that*." She does her best to laugh it off. *Thank goodness. For a second there I thought she had me.*

"But Shelby wrote the book." I nod as I say it. "That's the secret she was about to spill the night she was killed, wasn't it? That's why Shelby told Luke that the truth was going to come out and you wouldn't like it."

Ginger's face bleaches out of all color.

Oh wow, she knows. She'll tell everyone—I'll lose everything. The whole world will know I'm a fraud.

I shake my head at her. "The whole world is going to know you're a killer."

"What?" Her eyes bug out in horror. *There's no way she just read my mind. I must have said that out loud.* Her fingers float to her lips as if to conceal any more truths from seeping out.

I take a bold step forward. "Chelsea said the three of you took a safety course together at the range with Nessa." My adrenaline picks up and I begin to pant.

"So?" She eyes the door to the ballroom.

"You knew how to handle a gun. Not just any gun—the same gun you used to kill Shelby with."

Ginger takes a stumbling step backward as she staggers toward the woods and I'm quick to follow.

The air grows cold and damp and our breath crystalizes in long, papery plumes.

"Ginger, you asked me to put your things underneath the counter tonight. You knew that's where Nessa kept her purse that night, didn't you?"

She takes a breath and shakes her head in horror as she backs into the woods.

"You took Nessa's gun and killed Shelby, then placed it right back where you found it. Did you wipe your prints? Were you wearing gloves? You had thought about it, after all. This was no accident, was it?"

"You don't know what you're talking about." She turns and runs into the forest and I'm right there after her.

"Then why are you running?" I shout after her as I try to keep up pace.

Ginger stops short as she comes upon one of those oversized spider webs Jordy scattered throughout the woods to keep the guests from wandering into the endless labyrinth of evergreens.

"Get out of my way." Ginger barrels past me and tries her best to exit the woods, only to hit one dead end after another. "What the heck is wrong with this place?" Her voice thunders through the forest with an echo.

Fish jumps up between us, and Ginger lets out a sharp yelp.

"Oh goodness, that *thing* scared me." She cranes her neck past me as Sherlock and Peanut scamper this way. "What is this? The pet parade?"

Peanut gives a few aggressive barks. *Let me know when you want me to bite her ankles, Bizzy. It's been a long time coming, and it'll be a pleasure to do it.*

"Fine." Ginger tosses her hands in the air. "I killed her. I killed

Shelby right here at your stupid inn because she couldn't keep her ridiculous mouth shut. If you think I'm a piece of work, you should have known Shelby. Now she was a real witch with a capital everything. Of course, she wrote my book. And if she were smart, she would have kept that little tidbit to herself. I was giving her a share of profits under the table. But Shelby came from money. She didn't need it or crave it. The only thing she craved was power."

"You're right." My breathing is uneven. "She made Chelsea take the fall for the jewelry she stole. She made sure Scout and her aunt kept quiet about the thefts she was responsible for at the open houses. Did she threaten you, too?"

"*Ha!*" Ginger belts it out so loud, her voice shoots straight to the moon. "She knew better. I'm no amateur. With me, her power lay in actually pulling off the threat. She wanted to *humiliate* me." The veins in her neck distend as she says it. Her red hair shines like fire under the duress of a paper-white moon. "She was about to pull the plug on everything I've worked for. I'm sure it's what she was aiming for all along. The only thing she cared about was her persona, her fans. She wanted them to see how wonderful she was. She wanted them to feel pity once they found out that I took advantage of her—and she was going to make sure of it. Shelby thought it was going to propel her to new heights—and in a way she was right. That is, if you believe in the afterlife." Her left eye twitches. "Do you believe in the afterlife, Bizzy?" She takes a careful step forward. "Because if you do, I'd make peace with your maker right about now."

Ginger lunges forward as her hands collapse around my neck like a vise grip and we tumble to the ground.

Bizzy! Fish gives a spastic cry.

Oh, Bizzy! Peanut wails. ***Don't let her kill you, too. Do something!*** He pauses to glance to his left. ***Get in there, Sherlock. Stop this madness.*** He lets out a sharp bark, and soon Sherlock is right there with him as they do their best to attack her.

Fish leaps through the air and lands on Ginger's back and she flinches long enough for me to get out of her stranglehold.

I gasp for air as I try to crawl from beneath her.

"Would you stop, you dirty little mutt!" She jerks her knee and Peanut rolls across the forest floor like a bowling ball.

"Sherlock." I gag on his name. "Get Jasper." It comes out just above a whisper as my throat tries to recover from the death grip Ginger had on it.

Sherlock takes off, but Ginger doesn't miss a beat. She picks up a jagged rock twice the size of her hand and holds it precariously over my head.

"If only you hadn't pried." Her chest heaves with every word. "This is all your fault, Bizzy. You could have lived. I wouldn't have to kill again. Nessa wanted Shelby dead as much as I did. I practically did her a favor."

"And if you kill me? Who will you blame this time?" My voice quivers as I say it. Honestly? I had better not die. As far as last words go, those might go down as the worst.

Her chest rumbles with a quiet laugh. "The party is rife with monsters. I'm just one of them."

She lifts the rock a notch, and out from the lowest evergreen bough sails a flying miniature pirate with a tiny sword and fierce looking fangs that can do some real damage.

Fish lands right smack on Ginger's head, and I don't wait to see how this fantastical scenario plays out. Instead, I jab my foot into her gut and send her toppling backward as her hands try to work my tiny kitten out of her hair.

I land over Ginger with a thud just as the sound of heavy footfalls stampede in this direction.

"*Freeze!*" a male voice riots from our right, and I look up to see Detective Jasper Wilder with his weapon drawn, his jaw redefining itself with what looks like rage. "Leo, cuff her," he thunders.

Leo Granger falls to his knees, and before I know it, Jasper pulls me to him and his arms are tight around me.

"Bizzy Baker." Jasper plants a feverish kiss over my ear. "You gave me one hell of a scare. Are you okay? Are you hurt?"

"I'm fine," I pant. "Ginger confessed. She confessed to killing Shelby. She told me everything." I glance back at Ginger lying on her stomach with her wrists cuffed together behind her back. "It's over, isn't it?"

Jasper rubs my back and warms me. "It's over." His glowing gray eyes press into mine. "You're safe, Bizzy. That's all that matters." Jasper lands a tender kiss over my lips, slow and lingering, before diving into something far deeper, something that says we're official in a far better way than words.

My heart thumps wildly into my chest, and as horrific as this night has been, a part of me wants to remember this moment forever.

Justice for Shelby.

True love for me.

It's not a bad night, after all.

CHAPTER 20

*H*alloween has always been one of my favorite holidays for so many reasons, but the true lure was the ability to transform myself into someone or something else entirely—the donning of a costume, a mask. It allows you to walk around in someone else's skin for a single magical night.

All morning the Country Cottage Inn has indulged its guests in the haunted splendor that only this day can bring. The Cottage Café has served a themed menu all day long starting with pumpkin spice pancakes, pumpkin oatmeal, pumpkin scones, pumpkin French toast, and Emmie even fried up some donuts and glazed them in yellow, white, and orange stripes to make them look like candy corn. There are mummy wrapped hot dogs, spaghetti molded to look like brains, deviled eggs, stuffed jack-o-lantern bell peppers, spicy pumpkin chili, and dirt pudding for dessert.

I really do love Halloween, but if I'm being perfectly honest, I always feel a touch of relief once it's over. As hauntingly exhilarating as the fright fest of a day can be, my soul takes a breather knowing the cheeriest holiday of them all is right around the corner. Christmas.

And I'm breathing a sigh of relief a little early this year as well.

Ginger King was arrested and booked for the murder of Shelby Harris.

I still find it hard to imagine that Ginger would go as far as evicting someone off the planet to keep her ego from being deflated. She's about to learn the hard way that there could have been a much more amicable way to handle things.

Nessa was immediately released upon Ginger's arrest, and all charges against her were dropped. I told her to take as much time off from the inn as she needed. As elated as she is, there is still so much to process on her end as well.

The sun is getting ready to set on this, the last day of what has been a dizzying October, and Jasper asked me to meet him out on walkway just past the Cottage Café.

He strides over, looking sharp and heart-stopping in every capacity, with both Peanut and Sherlock by his side.

Fish jumps out of the bushes, sending both of the dogs barking and running toward the water, and Jasper and I share a warm laugh at the sight.

"Bizzy Baker." He lifts a brow as he takes me in. He's so cuttingly handsome that just looking at him makes my stomach bisect with heat. "You make a mighty fine looking innkeeper. Can I request that uniform be worn each and every day—and every night we're together?"

I give a little curtsy in my black and white short fitted dress. "I'm a French maid. And just so you know, this happens to be my standby costume I pull out once a year. So yes, there is a very strong chance you'll see it again." My cheeks heat in an instant. "I mean, that is if you're, you know, at the inn, or something like that."

Jasper's lucent gray eyes bear hard into mine. There's a smile flirting on his lips, but he's too stubborn to give it.

"Mind if we take a walk by the water?"

"I'd love to."

Jasper takes my hand as we head for the sand and a crisp autumn breeze picks up, making me wish I had opted for a coat. But the last thing I wanted was for Jasper to miss out on this bustier that makes my body look as if it's something you purchase from a box by Mattel. There's a reason I only wear this corseted contraption once a year, and breathing has something to do with it.

All right, fine. Emmie might have tightened it a notch because she knew Jasper and I were about to have the *talk*, and I foolishly let her put my respiration in peril for a man.

The Atlantic Ocean is roaring and angry, a vastness of steely gray water bucking and writhing as the surf pounds over the shore with a marked aggression. Jasper pauses just as we hit the damp sand and pulls me in.

"As you know, that talk I was having with Camila at the party ended abruptly, but this morning we were able to finish it. I made it clear as crystal that the two of us are over for good. I let her know we could be friends and nothing more." His lips cinch tight and tiny comma-like dimples erupt on either side of his cheeks. "I also let her know that I've given my heart to someone new." His eyes widen just a notch. "And that you and I were excited to see where the future takes us. I asked her to be respectful of that."

"Wow." My chest palpitates as I struggle to catch my breath. "Thank you. And by the way, I am extremely excited to have a future with you."

A crooked grin hikes up on his face as he nods. "Then we're together."

"We're together."

A choir of barking erupts around us as Sherlock and Peanut offer up their unanimous approval.

Fish scampers this way and lets out a sweet meow.

I've always liked him, Bizzy. Does this mean we can keep him? He can sleep on that tiny bed you bought me. I've never used it. It's as good as new.

A laugh bubbles from me. It's true. Fish sleeps right on top of my head, and it's often her tail swatting me over the face that wakes me up far before my alarm ever goes off.

But I won't be offering Jasper a place on my floor.

He's already got a place in my heart.

He leans in and the warmth of his cologne permeates me. "Do French maids charge for kisses, or am I confusing them for another profession entirely?"

I give his ribs a quick pinch. "They don't charge if you're their boyfriend."

"I guess I'm lucky then."

"I guess you are." I pull back for a moment and give him the once-over in his tweed jacket and jeans. "Hey? You didn't dress up today."

"I sure did. I'm a big, bad, scary detective, and I've got the gun and badge to prove it."

"Do you have the cuffs? Rumor has it, there is an extremely naughty French maid running around the inn."

His lids hood low as he scours my outfit with his eyes. "I'd better look into it. But fair warning—I might have to haul her over to my cottage for further interrogation."

I bite down playfully on my lower lip. "Don't let her get away with anything. I hear she's very wily."

"I'll make sure to give her exactly what she deserves."

Jasper lands his lips to mine and we indulge in all the kisses we want, for free.

HALLOWEEN NIGHT AT THE HAUNTED HARVEST FESTIVAL IS WHERE all of Cider Cove has decided to congregate, according to the wild turnout. There are witches and goblins of every shape and size as kids young and old take over the fairgrounds hyped on far too much candy and cider.

Clouds hang heavy in the violet sky, and every now and again they part ways, allowing the full moon to inspect the happy chaos ensuing below.

A large banner that reads *Happy Falloween!* hangs over the dessert table Emmie and I just refreshed with baskets of pumpkin spice mini muffins. Judging by the way we've been selling out at the café, they were a very big hit.

Jasper pops up next to me, holding up two large black tickets with orange print that reads *good for one haunted hayride.*

"We're in." He lands a kiss to my lips. "They said to come back in an hour when the line dies down."

"Perfect. I hope it's good and scary. Have I mentioned that I need to be held extra tight when I'm afraid?"

A crooked grin expands over his lips. "This is going to be one terrifying night."

"That's what I'm counting on. Speaking of tonight"—I offer him a cheeky grin—"I believe you owe me takeout at your place. Nessa is innocent. I won our little bet."

"You at my place for takeout? I'm the clear winner here. In fact, I'm getting hungry already." His lips twitch with devilish intent and his lids hang low. My guess is food is at the bottom of the list of the things he's hungry for.

"Bizzy!" a bright and cheery female voice calls from the left and we turn to find Nessa Crosby dressed as an angel in a cute short white dress, a pair of billowy feathered wings that has more of a naughty runway appeal than anything truly angelic, and she even has a gold glittering halo strapped to her head.

"Nessa, you look amazing." I pull her in for a nice, long hug.

"I thought I'd try to drive the point home for the people who still might think I had anything to do with this."

"Don't worry, Nessa," Jasper is quick to comfort her. "You're free and clear, and your record won't be marred by this."

"Believe me, I'm thankful." She shrugs. "But I might don the halo straight through the new year just to shut down the naysayers at the inn. And speaking of the inn"—she looks my way —"rumor has it, there's an adorable little puppy who still hasn't found his forever home. I know that Shelby and I didn't exactly get along, but I'd love to have Peanut if you'll let me. I've never fallen in love so hard and fast before. And with everything he's gone through, I'll do my best to make it up to him."

I glance to Jasper. "I don't see why not. But only if you promise to bring him around the inn now and again. I think Sherlock and Fish will really miss him."

"You bet." Her eyes brighten. "In fact, I'll make sure you see him more often than not. He's so great with people and he truly deserves to have a family of his own."

"I agree," I say. "I'll be heading back to the inn later tonight to relieve Grady, and I'll be sure to pull out the blanket and toys I have for Peanut."

"Perfect. I'll swing by on my way home. I can't wait to spoil that sweet little baby boy. He's going to have a great life."

"I know he will."

She takes off, and an odd sight at the hot apple cider booth has me doing a double take. A part of me isn't sure I want to bring it to Jasper's attention. You know what they say, let sleeping dogs lie.

Jasper glances back and sighs once he sees it. "I know about them," he whispers.

My mouth falls open as I follow his gaze right back to where Jordy and Camila share a quick laugh.

"I guess Jordy is interested." I shrug. "Can't say I blame him. She's a beautiful woman."

Jasper's chest bucks with a silent laugh. "The interior doesn't always match the exterior. Let's hope she goes easy on the poor guy."

I'm about to look away just as Leo and Mack step their way, and the four of them start in on a conversation together.

"You know"—I shake my head—"there are some couple

cliques I just don't want to be a part of."

"Hear, hear. I think this is a good time to make a run for the funnel cake."

"Or the haunted maze. Rumor has it, there are a lot of places to steal a moment of privacy."

We take off in that direction, only to bump into a trio of familiar faces—Georgie, Macy, and Emmie.

Georgie holds her arms open wide, only to reveal she has three additional sets of arms sewn to her kaftan and it has an unnerving human spider effect.

"Well, boo to you, too," she sings as she pulls us both into a warm embrace. "Where are you kids off to? Let me guess. You're off to get a room at the inn." She elbows me in the ribs while offering a cheeky wink.

Macy balks as she looks to Jasper, "*Please*. My sister only pretends to be a naughty girl on Halloween." Her black painted lips smear an ironic smile. "As soon as the clock strikes twelve, you'll find out it was all hocus-pocus."

Jasper's cheek flinches. "So you're saying there's still time."

A riotous bout of laughter breaks out from our little circle.

Emmie leans in. "Just FYI, Detective Wilder. That's my best friend's heart you're holding. If you break it, you'll have to answer to me. I've got a can of pepper spray, and I'm not afraid to use it." She grimaces. "Okay, so I'm totally terrified to use the pepper spray. Just don't do anything stupid for both of our sakes."

Jasper nods her way. "Duly noted."

"Ignore the threats," I say, wrapping an arm around his waist. "Her bark is worse than her bite."

"Not mine," Georgie is quick to counter. "My bark is just as bad as my bite. Throw one of those hot Wilder brothers my way and I'll be glad to demonstrate."

Macy groans as she spots something just past my shoulder. "Incoming hot brother—attached to a rather witchy preppy."

I turn around to see Mom and Max headed this way. They're

holding hands and look adorably like the perfect couple. I guess Mom hasn't tossed Max out on his ear yet in lieu of a little extra sleep.

They say a quick hello.

Mom leans in. "Enjoy the festivities, kids. Starting at midnight, they'll be shoving the next holiday down our throats."

Macy's chest pumps with a silent laugh. "Mom, you are forever a cheery point of light."

Georgie raises all eight of her hands. "Next holiday? That must mean it's time to leapfrog over the turkey. And who the heck cares? I love Christmas. I love the way all of Cider Cove is transformed into a winter wonderland."

Emmie nods. "I love strolling through Candy Cane Lane. They have a contest every year to see who can do the most over-the-top decorations, and each year it gets crazier and crazier. I hear one of the houses will have a light show set to music and everything."

Mom rolls her eyes. "Oh, goody," she moans. "I hope they turn up the volume nice and loud so the entire town can hear it."

Georgie lifts a finger. "Now you're thinking."

Macy wrinkles her nose. "I really miss those old-fashioned Christmases when all of us would get together—you know, the Crosbys and the Bakers."

Georgie shoves a fist in the air. "And the Conners."

"And the Conners, what?" Dad asks as he and Gwyneth emerge from the shadows.

Dad looks handsome, yet boyish, a running theme in his life. And Gwyneth looks sharp in a crisp black leather jacket with her hair slicked back and dark cherry wine lipstick slashed over her mouth.

They each have an arm wrapped around one another's waist, and both Jasper and I exchange a quick glance.

I clear my throat. "I was just about to extend an invitation to everyone here to attend the inn's very first old-fashioned

Christmas Eve dinner. I realize it's still months away, but I figure I'd plant the seed and hopefully convince you all to come out."

"Yes!" Emmie cries out. "We'll have the Cottage Café cater. And Bizzy and I will come up with an amazing dessert menu."

Macy makes a face. "As long as you keep Bizzy from doing the actual baking."

Georgie leans in. "You mean *burning*."

And the entire lot of them has a laugh at my expense. Heck, I laugh, too.

Dad gives a firm whistle and garners our attention in no time flat.

"Since you're all here, Gwyneth and I have an announcement we'd like to make—surprisingly, it's about Christmas Eve as well." He shrugs over at her and she shrugs right back. "In fact, I think we'd both be open to hosting the event at the inn so none of you would have to change any plans."

"What event?" My heart thumps unnaturally because I'm pretty sure I'm not going to like it.

Dad takes a quick breath as he looks around to everyone in our circle.

"Gwyneth and I are getting married."

An explosion of confusion breaks out—with the exception of Georgie who has decided this is the perfect time to offer a celebratory howl at the moon, forcing our small circle to break apart in an effort to save our eardrums. My dad and Gwyneth pretty much shot our sanity out for the night.

Jasper pulls me to the side. "Don't worry, Bizzy. I'm on this. In fact, I'll take care of it right now." He takes off in their direction before I can wish him luck. Something tells me he'll need far more than that. He might need a crucifix and some holy water to stop this heretical catastrophe from happening. My father and his mother are a train wreck in any capacity.

I'm about to head over to my sister and Emmie when a dark-haired, smoldering beauty steps in my path.

"Hello, Camila," I say, lacking the proper enthusiasm. And as much as I'd like to thank my father and his eager-to-be bride for my morose mood, I have a feeling the vixen before me has something to do with it, too. There's something about that smirk on her face that lets me know we're still very much locking horns over Jasper.

"Bizzy." Her lips curl with dangerous intent. "I suppose Jasper told you about our little talk. Congratulations, by the way." Her left brow hooks into her forehead as if she were amused.

"Thank you. We're excited about the future."

"Oh, you should be." The whites of her eyes glint under the duress of the lights strung up along the booths to our right. "You should be very excited about getting to know Jasper. He's a very exciting man." She shrugs, her dark eyes digging deeper into mine.

But he's not as exciting as you, is he, Bizzy?

My own eyes widen a notch and a dark laugh strums from her.

That's right. I've figured out your little secret. You see, I've known about Leo's abilities all along. It's what drew me to him to begin with—that captivating feeling that this gorgeous man was somehow always in the know. Always capable of hijacking my next thought. Of course, I was able to pull it out of him quite easily. She hikes a shoulder. *A woman does know how to get certain things from a man, doesn't she, Bizzy?* She openly frowns at me. *What do you think Jasper would do if he found out about your special ability?* She rolls her eyes. *I guess we'll find out when the time comes. And what do you think the government would do if they found out about the neat little party trick you have up your proverbial sleeve?*

My fingers float to my lips in horror. Camila is like a train wreck I can't look away from.

I bet they would be very interested to speak to you, Bizzy Baker. In fact, I bet you'll be far too busy—an irony I will never get enough of—once they cart you off to some government testing facility for good. I'm sure they have a special division for people of your talent. What do you think? Russian spy? I bet you'll be traveling abroad quite a bit. That is, if they let you out of your holding cell.

I clear my throat. "Why are you staring at me?"

She belts out a laugh. *Nice try, Bizzy. Has that line worked for you before?*

She looks to her left and I follow her gaze to where Jasper seems to be having a rather animated discussion with both his mother and his brother, Max.

Camila steps over and effectively blocks my view of them. *Of course, there is a way to avoid that whole awful mess. I'm thinking a rather abrupt breakup is in the cards for the two of you.* She bleeds a dark smile my way once again. *Jasper is mine, Bizzy. And don't you ever forget it.*

She takes off, and I watch as she makes her way back to Jordy.

Camila has staked her claim to Jasper and driven her spear right through my heart in the process.

If Camila wants a war, she'll get one.

And I have a feeling my relationship with Jasper might be the very first casualty.

*NEED MORE CIDER COVE? PICK UP SANTA CLAWS CALAMITY (Country Cottage Mysteries 3) NOW!

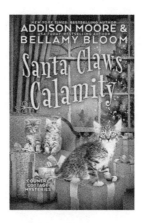

My name is Bizzy Baker, and I can read minds—not every mind, not every *time* but most of the time and believe me when I say it's not all it's cracked up to be.

It's Christmas in Cider Cove and it's time for the annual house decorating competition. But on the night set to determine the winner, the residents of Candy Cane Lane get more than they bargained for. They don't just get an award—they get murder.

BIZZY BAKER RUNS THE COUNTRY COTTAGE INN, HAS THE ABILITY to pry into the darkest recesses of both the human and animal mind, and has just stumbled upon a body. With the help of her kitten, *Fish*, a mutt named Sherlock Bones and an ornery yet dangerously good looking homicide detective, Bizzy is determined to find the killer.

CIDER COVE, MAINE IS THE PREMIERE DESTINATION FOR FUN AND relaxation. But when a body turns up, it's the premiere destination for murder.

*Don't miss it! Pick up Santa Claws Calamity (Country Cottage Mysteries 3) NOW!

RECIPE

COUNTRY COTTAGE CAFÉ

Pumpkin Spice Mini Muffins

Hello everyone! It's me, Bizzy Baker! The Country Cottage Café has an amazing recipe for pumpkin spice mini muffins and I just have to share it with you. As you know, I'm a bit of a disaster in the kitchen but my best friend Emmie knows how to whip out a top notch treat that will be a crowd pleaser every time. And that's exactly why she's in charge of the kitchen at the Country Cottage Café. You must try these mini muffins. They are to die for. Jasper and I cannot get enough of their pumpkin spice goodness.

Happy eating!
    XOXO ~ Bizzy

1 ½ cup all-purpose flour
    ¾ cup sugar
    5 tbs butter
    2 tsp baking powder
    2 eggs
    2 tsp vanilla

1 tsp cinnamon
¼ tsp nutmeg
¼ tsp ground cloves
¼ tsp ground ginger
¼ salt
1 cup pumpkin puree
½ cup evaporated milk

Preheat oven to 375°
Line a mini muffin pan with paper pastry cups
Add into a mixing bowl sifted flour, sugar, cinnamon, ginger, nutmeg, cloves, baking powder, and salt. Cut butter into the bowl until crumbled.

In an additional mixing bowl add pumpkin puree, evaporated milk, eggs and vanilla. Add pumpkin mixture in with flour mixture and incorporate.

Bake for 15-20 minutes until you can insert a toothpick and it pulls away clean from center.

*yields about 24 mini muffins or 12 standard size muffins.

Serve warm and enjoy!

BOOKS BY ADDISON MOORE

Paranormal Women's Fiction
Hot Flash Homicides
Midlife in Glimmerspell
Wicked in Glimmerspell
Mistletoe in Glimmerspell

Cozy Mysteries

Cruising Through Midlife
Cruising Through Midlife
Mai Tai Murder Cruise
Hibiscus Homicide Cruise

Brambleberry bay Murder Club
Brambleberry Bay Murder Club

Cozy Mysteries

Meow for Murder
Murder at Mortimer Manor
Murder Old School
Socialite's Guide to Murder
Haunted Halloween Murder
Murder for Christmas
Murder Made Delicious
Marriage can be Murder

Country Cottage Mysteries

Kittyzen's Arrest

Dog Days of Murder

Santa Claws Calamity

Bow Wow Big House

Murder Bites

Felines and Fatalities

A Killer Tail

Cat Scratch Cleaver

Just Buried

Butchered After Bark

A Frightening Fangs-giving

A Christmas to Dismember

Sealed with a Hiss

A Winter Tail of Woe

Lock, Stock, and Feral

Itching for Justice

Raining Cats and Killers

Death Takes a Holiday

Copycat Killer Thriller

Happy Howl-o-ween Horror

Twas the Night Before Murder

Smitten Kitten Corruption

Cruising for Trouble

Beach Body

A Ruthless Ruff Patch

Murder in the Mix Mysteries

Cutie Pies and Deadly Lies

Bobbing for Bodies

Pumpkin Spice Sacrifice

Gingerbread & Deadly Dread

Seven-Layer Slayer

Red Velvet Vengeance

Bloodbaths and Banana Cake

New York Cheesecake Chaos

Lethal Lemon Bars

Macaron Massacre

Wedding Cake Carnage

Donut Disaster

Toxic Apple Turnovers

Killer Cupcakes

Pumpkin Pie Parting

Yule Log Eulogy

Pancake Panic

Sugar Cookie Slaughter

Devil's Food Cake Doom

Snickerdoodle Secrets

Strawberry Shortcake Sins

Cake Pop Casualties

Flag Cake Felonies

Peach Cobbler Confessions

Poison Apple Crisp

Spooky Spice Cake Curse

Pecan Pie Predicament

Eggnog Trifle Trouble

Waffles at the Wake

Raspberry Tart Terror

Baby Bundt Cake Confusion

Chocolate Chip Cookie Conundrum

Wicked Whoopie Pies

Key Lime Pie Perjury

Red, White, and Blueberry Muffin Murder

Honey Buns Homicide

Apple Fritter Fright

Vampire Brownie Bite Bereavement

Pumpkin Roll Reckoning

Cookie Exchange Execution

Heart-Shaped Confection Deception

Birthday Cake Bloodshed

Cream Puff Punishment

Last Rites Beignet Bites

Christmas Fudge Fatality

Murder in the Mix Boxed Set
Murder in the Mix (Books 1-3)

Mystery
Little Girl Lost
Never Say Sorry
The First Wife's Secret

Romance
Just Add Mistletoe

For list of more books please visit addisonmoore.com

ACKNOWLEDGMENTS

Thank you, the reader, for coming along on this amazing journey with us! We hope you love Cider Cove as much as we do. We are SUPER excited to share the next book with you, **Santa Claws Calamity**! It's beginning to look a lot like murder. Thank you from the bottom of our hearts for taking this roller coaster ride with us. We cannot wait to take you on the next leg of the adventure.

Special thank you to the following people for taking care of this book—Kaila Eileen Turingan-Ramos, Kathryn Jacoby, Jodie Tarleton, Lisa Markson, Ashley Marie Daniels and Margaret Lapointe. And a very big shout out to Lou Harper for designing the world's best covers.

A heartfelt thank you to Paige Maroney Smith for being so amazing.

And last, but never least, thank you to Him who sits on the throne. Worthy is the Lamb! Glory and honor and power are yours. We owe you everything, Jesus.

ABOUT THE AUTHORS

Addison Moore is a *New York Times, USA Today,* and *Wall Street Journal* bestselling author. Her work has been featured in *Cosmopolitan* Magazine. Previously she worked as a therapist on a locked psychiatric unit for nearly a decade. She resides on the West Coast with her husband, four wonderful children, and two dogs where she eats too much chocolate and stays up way too late. When she's not writing, she's reading. Addison's Celestra Series has been optioned for film by **20th Century Fox.**

Bellamy Bloom is a *USA TODAY* bestselling author who writes cozy mysteries filled with humor, intrigue and a touch of the supernatural. When she's not writing up a murderous storm she's snuggled by the fire with her two precious pooches, chewing down her to-be-read pile and drinking copious amounts of coffee.

Made in the USA
Las Vegas, NV
24 December 2024

15321108R00132